She had to be working at The Bluffs...

But there was no denying Becca wanted to see Dr. David Bryson. She liked his voice. Or perhaps had been mesmerized by it. Rich, with a whisper of heartbreak.

Now she sounded like a guide giving a spiel to tourists! The simple truth was the man was a recluse who dressed in black and came out of his fortress only at night. And she had agreed to go to his castle like some poor lamb to slaughter.

The only thing to do was call in the morning and back out.

I need you, Becca.

The words slammed into her senses, and her heart thundered in her chest. The voice of David Bryson haunted her. Smooth, mysterious. Seductive.

She'd have to make tomorrow's visit. If only to satisfy her own curiosity and convince herself that Dr. David Bryson was just a man with no power over her.

Dear Harlequin Intrigue Reader,

May holds more mayhem for you in this action-packed month of terrific titles.

Patricia Rosemoor revisits her popular series THE McKENNA LEGACY in this first of a two-book miniseries. Irishman Curran McKenna has a gift for gentling horses—and the ladies. But Thoroughbred horse owner Jane Grantham refuses to be tamed—especially when she is guarding not only her heart, but secrets that could turn deadly. Will she succumb to this *Mysterious Stranger*?

Bestselling author Joanna Wayne delivers the final book in our MORIAH'S LANDING in-line continuity series. In *Behind the Veil*, we finally meet the brooding recluse Dr. David Bryson. Haunted for years by his fiancée's death, he meets a new woman in town who wants to teach him how to love again. But when she is targeted as a killer's next victim, David will use any means necessary to make sure that history doesn't repeat itself.

The Bride and the Mercenary continues Harper Allen's suspenseful miniseries THE AVENGERS. For two years Ainslie O'Connor believed that the man she'd passionately loved—Seamus Malone—was dead. But then she arrives at her own society wedding, only to find that her dead lover is still alive! Will Seamus's memory return in time to save them both?

And finally, we are thrilled to introduce a brand-new author—Lisa Childs. You won't want to miss her very first book *Return of the Lawman*—with so many twists and turns, it will keep you guessing…and looking for more great stories from her!

Happy reading,

Denise O'Sullivan
Associate Senior Editor
Harlequin Intrigue

BEHIND THE VEIL
JOANNA WAYNE

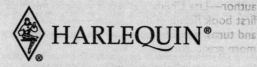

HARLEQUIN®

TORONTO • NEW YORK • LONDON
AMSTERDAM • PARIS • SYDNEY • HAMBURG
STOCKHOLM • ATHENS • TOKYO • MILAN • MADRID
PRAGUE • WARSAW • BUDAPEST • AUCKLAND

Special thanks and acknowledgment are given to Joanna Wayne for her contribution to the MORIAH'S LANDING series.

ISBN 0-373-22662-4

BEHIND THE VEIL

Printed in U.S.A.

ABOUT THE AUTHOR

Joanna Wayne lives with her husband just a few miles from steamy, exciting New Orleans, but her home is the perfect writer's hideaway. A lazy bayou, complete with graceful herons, colorful wood ducks and an occasional alligator, winds just below her back garden. When not creating tales of spine-tingling suspense and heartwarming romance, she enjoys reading, traveling, playing golf and spending time with family and friends.

Joanna believes that one of the special joys of writing is knowing that her stories have brought enjoyment to or somehow touched the lives of her readers. You can write Joanna at P.O. Box 2851, Harvey, LA 70059-2851.

Books by Joanna Wayne

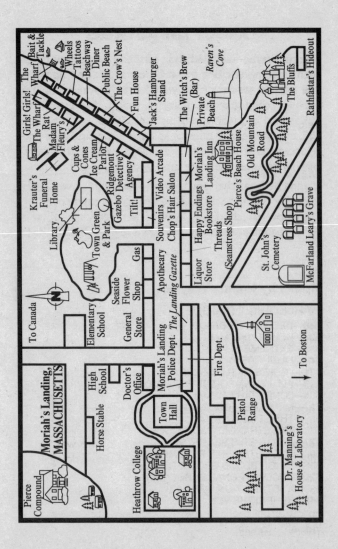

CAST OF CHARACTERS

Becca Smith—She's intrigued by the mysterious recluse who lives in the castle on top of the cliff, but will her attraction for him lead her into a killer's trap?

Dr. David Bryson—Tortured by the loss of his beloved fiancée, he lives only to find the man responsible for the tragedy—until he meets Becca Smith.

Marley Glasglow—He's surly and bitter, and his opinions about David Bryson—none of them good— are set in stone.

Brie, Kat and Elizabeth—New friends of Becca's who were present the night Claire Cavendish was abducted.

Claire Cavendish—Becca's friend who is still mentally and emotionally unstable from her abduction and subsequent torture five years ago.

Kevin Pinelle—A happy-go-lucky young fisherman with an eye for the ladies.

Larry Gayle—A young male friend of Becca and Claire who thinks the town would be better off without David Bryson.

Shamus McManus—An old fisherman who knows a lot about what goes on in the wharf area.

Tasha Pierce—David Bryson's fiancée, who was killed in an explosion on the eve of their wedding.

Geoffrey Pierce—Tasha's uncle.

Carson Megham—A homicide detective hell-bent on capturing the killer who's terrifying the citizens of Moriah's Landing.

To Priscilla Berthiaume for putting together
the idea for this wonderful Gothic series, and to my
friends Amanda Stevens, B.J. Daniels and Dani Sinclair for
being such an agreeable, fun and talented group to work
with. A special thank-you to Dr. David Cavanaugh for
answering my endless questions. And to Wayne, always.

Prologue

Sweat beaded on the man's brow as he struggled to drag the lifeless body into the thick clump of bushes and untamed undergrowth. The stench of death punctuated the night air and clogged his nostrils, but he couldn't leave her like this. The job had to be done exactly according to plan.

Her leg caught on a rock, and he yanked it free, his hand brushing the delicate curve of her ankle as he did. She'd been an easy victim. Weak, innocent, gullible.

So easy. Almost too easy. He'd expected it to be more of a challenge, more satisfying to watch life seep from her body when he'd strangled her, watch blood gush from the two slashes that had severed her arteries. Instead it was over so quickly, he barely had time to appreciate the perfection of his work.

Just like it had been done twenty years ago. And, like twenty years ago, the stupid Moriah's Landing police would never solve the murders. There had been four then, but only three remained unsolved and attributed to the serial killer. He'd probably stop at three now, as well. Or maybe he wouldn't stop at all.

He took the knife, ran his gloved fingers along the

edge of the blade, and then plunged it once more into the cold, pale flesh.

Easy. Easy. Easy. And perfect. Only one thing left to do. Working meticulously, he carved an *M* and an *L* into her abdomen. Something new to make certain everyone knew that McFarland Leary had returned.

Chapter One

Rebecca Smith snipped the emerald thread, laid her scissors on the table and held up the full satin dress for a critical look at the finished garment. The fabric swished as it fell into iridescent folds, catching the glow of the bright overhead lights.

Standing, she held it to her shoulders and took a few twirls around the room. It was the first piece of clothing she'd made for herself in months, but she'd outdone herself this time. The fabric was fabulous, the color rich, the sheen almost glittery.

Stopping to admire the finished creation in front of the full-length mirror, she could almost imagine herself attending a ball in old England. It would be the perfect dress for the Fall Extravaganza. On that night the town of Moriah's Landing would be transported back in time, to the way it had been the year it was first inhabited. The night would be magical, a celebration that would hopefully dispel the sense of danger and fear that prevailed every fifth year when McFarland Leary was said to rise from the grave. If everything went as planned, tourists from miles around would flock into the narrow streets to celebrate the town's three hundred and fiftieth anniversary year in a spectacular evening of dancing, vignettes, music and food.

If all went as planned, they would return to their homes when the festivities were over—alive.

The dress slipped through Becca's fingers, and she barely caught it before it fell to the floor of the shop. The uneasy feeling that had lurked just beneath her consciousness all day had leapt to the forefront, icy and onerous and threatening to squeeze the life from her lungs.

She hated these moments when she seemed to slip into the depths of some world far beyond the one she knew as a simple seamstress. She never told anyone about these experiences, the same way she never admitted that she was anyone but Rebecca Smith, a young woman with simple values and meager expectations. It was better this way, made her less of an oddity, gave people no reason to pity her or to speculate about her past.

She laid the dress across the worktable, then walked to the front window and stared into the grayness of twilight. The streetlights had come on along Main Street, tiny globes of illumination, blurred and dulled by the thick fog that coated the air. A black car pulled up in front of the liquor store next door and a tall man in a pair of worn jeans and a windbreaker climbed from the passenger side of the car and sauntered to the entrance. He nodded and waved when he caught sight of her watching through the window. She waved back.

Moriah's Landing was ordinarily a quiet, safe town in spite of the popular tales of witches and warlocks and ghosts who rose from their graves to kill innocent women. She didn't believe in such nonsense, anyway. Humans committed murders, and though the town of Moriah's Landing had experienced its share of those, there was no reason to believe that evil still lurked in dark graveyards or strolled the rocky beaches at midnight.

No reason at all, unless you believed the legend of McFarland Leary, a man who'd been dead for centuries and still rose from the grave every five years to torture and kill innocent females.

Or if you bought into the stories that circulated about the monster on the hill. She closed her eyes, and the image of a lean, brooding man with swarthy skin and dark, piercing eyes walked through her mind. Thick hair fell across his forehead and hung past his ears, only half hiding the nasty scar that crawled down the right side of his face.

Dr. David Bryson. Living in the Bluffs, his formidable castle of stone and menacing turrets, guarded by hideous, lifeless gargoyles that bared rusted teeth and sharpened claws.

When she thought of danger and foreboding, his was always the face that appeared in her mind, and still the man intrigued her. She'd asked questions of all her friends, listened to the talk about him, watched for him, half hoping he'd materialize from the shadows when she walked home by herself after dark.

She'd spotted him one night just as she'd finished turning the key to lock the shop door. He'd been standing at the corner near her shop. She'd looked him straight in the eye, studied his features in the faint glow of the streetlight. Her heart had beat erratically, but she'd stood as if frozen to the spot, mesmerized, drawn to the man half the town claimed was a mad murderer.

The jangling of the telephone jolted her from her thoughts. She took a deep breath and forced the image of Dr. Bryson from her mind before she answered. "Threads. How may I help you?"

"Becca, it's Larry Gayle. Some of us are heading over to the carnival tonight. Want to join us?"

She hesitated. "The weatherman is predicting thundershowers."

"Aw, come on. It's Friday night. Kat and Jonah are going, and if it rains, we'll duck into one of the bars along the wharf."

"In that case, count me in." She hadn't seen Kat nearly enough since her friend had fallen in love with and married Jonah. Jonah was with the FBI and Kat was one of the toughest private investigators around. Still, it had been a rough year for Kat. After twenty years, the man who'd killed her mother in Kat's presence had finally been arrested. The first of the infamous Moriah's Landing murders of twenty years ago had been solved. The last three had not.

"What time?" she asked, pushing thoughts of the murder aside.

"I'll pick you up about seven," Larry answered, "unless that's too soon."

Her gaze rose to the clock over the door. It was already a quarter after six, but it was only a ten-minute walk to the room she rented from the Cavendish family, and it wouldn't take long to slip into a pair of jeans and a sweatshirt. "I'll be ready."

A few minutes later, she'd straightened her work area, hung her dress on a hanger so that the wrinkles could fall out and turned out the lights in the shop. Pulling the door closed, she fit the key into the lock and turned it, checking before she walked away to make sure the lock had caught and held.

There was little breaking and entering in Moriah's

Landing, but it didn't hurt to be cautious, especially since she only managed the shop for the owner. One day she hoped to buy it, but for now she was content to have a job she enjoyed.

Picking up her pace, she turned off of Main Street and onto a narrow unlit side street. It was the one secluded area on her short walk home. It didn't really frighten her, but still she always picked up her pace when she started down it. The lots on either side of the road belonged to one of the Pierces, but they had never built here.

The wind blew in from the ocean, sharp and damp and prickling her flesh. Not a great night for a carnival, but she was relieved not to be staying home tonight. The chilling presence that had haunted her all day began to swell into an almost palpable sensation as she rounded the last corner and walked beneath a canopy of tree branches and shadows.

If she believed in witchcraft, she would fear she was one, and that the chill inside her predicted the imminence of danger or death.

If she believed. But she didn't.

DAVID BRYSON WALKED the rocky path along the edge of the craggy cliffs and stared down at the swirling water as it crashed against the treacherous rocks below. Once the sight had filled him with awe and excitement. Now it was only a bitter reminder that it was the place where he had lost his world.

Some claimed he'd also lost his sanity that horrible night five years ago, and perhaps they were the ones who understood best.

Instinctively, his hand moved to his face, and his fingers traced the jagged lines of the scar that ran from his right temple to below his ear. The facial disfiguration, his conspicuous limp and the hideous patches of coarse, red skin on his chest and stomach were always with him to remind him of the explosion.

Still, the plastic surgeons had worked wonders, rebuilt his face, transformed him from something so ghastly he couldn't bear to pass in front of a mirror to something merely hideous. The doctors had saved his life even while he'd begged them for the release of death. To this day, he'd never fully forgiven them.

"Dr. Bryson."

He turned at the sound of his name and located the lone figure standing behind the Bluffs. The man was no more than an outline in the deepening darkness, but David didn't have to see his butler to recognize him. He knew the voice well.

He waved and called up to him. "I'm down here, Richard."

David took one last look at the water below him, then tilted his face and examined the turbulent layers of dark clouds before starting back up the rocky path.

Too bad about the gathering storm, but if the carnies were lucky, it would hold off for a few hours. The carnival had been a highlight of the fall season for years, coming to town just after the students at the all-girls college of Heathrow had plunged into the sea of sorority activities and before they became immersed in serious studies.

Memories sneaked into his mind. A kiss at the top of the Ferris wheel, Tasha's body pressing into his as they spun on the Tilt-A-Whirl.

A ragged ache tore at his insides. He fought it by pushing his body to the limits, ignoring the stabbing pain in his right leg and jogging up the slippery path that ran along the edge of the cliff. In minutes, he'd covered the ground between him and Richard and stopped at the man's side.

"You risk your life when you do that, sir."

"What do you expect from a madman?"

"Indeed. You're no more mad than I am."

"You need to get out more, Richard. Mingle with the townspeople. They'll tell you what an insane monster you work for."

"I take no stock in the tales of people who walk around in fear that some old ghost is going to rise from the cemetery and kill their virgins."

"Ghost tales are good for tourism."

"They're the invention of superstitious fools. There's evil in this town, cruelty, too. But it doesn't come from ghosts or witches." Richard turned and started back toward the house. David followed him, wondering as always what he'd do without the man.

Richard Crawford had come to work for him five and a half years ago when David had returned to Moriah's Landing and purchased the Bluffs. Richard's hair had grayed around the ears since then and receded from his forehead, but he was still fit and youthful for a man who'd celebrate his sixtieth birthday this year.

More important, Richard was probably the only one who understood how much David still loved his dead fiancée. He missed Tasha's voice, her smile, the way she'd made him feel. She'd been so young and innocent. And beautiful.

"...dinner?"

"I'm sorry, Richard. Did you ask me a question?"

Richard turned and raised an eyebrow. "Is something the matter, sir?"

"I was just a bit preoccupied. Nothing new." He'd

told Richard repeatedly that he didn't need to refer to
him as sir, but the man was from the old school, and
even though he was as much friend and confidant as
servant, Richard always made certain to keep that defin-
ing edge of separation between them.

"I asked if you were ready for dinner," Richard re-
peated. "The cook's gone for the day, but she left everything in the oven. It will take me only a few minutes
to serve it."

"Dinner. I'd almost forgotten that we hadn't eaten."

"I think you would forget to eat entirely, sir, if someone weren't around to remind you."

"I might at that. It's my work that keeps me going
these days." His work and a new fascination, one that
frightened him even more than the impenetrable moods
that had almost destroyed him after Tasha's death. One
that he would never dare mention, not even to Richard.

"Will you be going out tonight, sir?"

"Maybe later. First I plan to go back to the lab and
work."

The question was ritual. The answer was automatic.
After dinner, he either went to his office in the dark
corridors beneath the rambling castle or to the test tubes
and microscopes that filled the west wing of the Bluffs.
He'd work until his mind was numb and fatigue robbed
him of the control that kept his inner demons in check.
Then he'd lose all perspective and turn into the madman
every one believed him to be.

He'd slip from the confines of the Bluffs and drive to
the edge of town. He'd park his car and walk the streets
and back alleys, searching endlessly for answers he
never found. One day he would. And when he did, revenge would be swift and unbelievably sweet.

Becca Smith was not part of the answers or the revenge. But lately, he'd ended up on her street far too often. Something about her haunted him, and try as he might, he couldn't seem to shake her from his mind.

Richard paused at the back door. "I hear the whole town is gearing up for the Fall Extravaganza. Perhaps you should go. One night of fun won't ruin your reputation as a serious scientist."

He touched his fingers to the scar. "I'd frighten the children."

"With one little scar? I seriously doubt that, sir."

"With one *ghastly* scar. I suppose I could dig out the mask I wore in the first years after the explosion and go as the Phantom."

"Just go as yourself. I predict you'll be pleasantly surprised."

David turned away. "Moriah's Landings has always had lots of surprises for me. Only one was ever pleasant, and in the end, it was the cruelest surprise of all."

"That was five years ago. Besides, test tubes make lonely bedfellows."

"True, but they never pull away in disgust when I stand in front of them."

David pushed through the door and stepped inside the bleak interior of the Bluffs. Nothing but grays and browns and thick, opaque draperies. Tasha had planned to redecorate the place, fill it with light and brighter fabrics to compliment the richness of the dark woods of the furniture.

Her plans had died with her. Without Tasha, there was no light. Besides, he'd lost all interest in the structure that had so intrigued him when he'd purchased it. Now he spent most of his days in the lab or out staring at the water breaking over the treacherous rocks at the foot of the jagged cliffs.

A bleak and isolated life. But a few miles away, the carnival was in full swing. Coeds' laughter, painted horses, music, a kaleidoscope of colors. And for the first time in five long years, he felt himself *almost* wishing he were part of it.

He closed his eyes for a second as Richard walked ahead of him toward the kitchen. He expected Tahsa's face to materialize in his mind, but this time it was the image of Becca Smith that danced behind his eyelids. Tall and willowy, her long blond hair falling around her shoulders.

He'd have to be very careful if he left the house tonight. And he knew he'd leave. The town was already beckoning.

"STEP RIGHT UP. All you have to do is break three plates to win a prize. Or give me the prize you have walking next to you, and I'll hand over all the stuffed bears I own." The hawker tipped a faded baseball cat at Becca as she and Larry walked past his booth.

"Keep your bears," Larry said. "I know a good thing when I see one." He grinned and wrapped his right arm around Becca's shoulder, slowing so that Kat and Jonah could catch up with them.

"Do you want a bear?" Jonah asked Kat. "I pitch a mean fastball."

"Let's see. A bear or a beer? I'll take a beer."

"Aw," the hawker groaned. "She's only kidding. Every woman wants a teddy bear. Or how about one of these cute pink cats? Come on, ladies. Help me out here."

A large drop of rain plopped on the tip of Becca's nose, the first of the evening. "Looks like our luck is running out," she said, quickly forgetting the hawker, who was already rescuing his best prizes from the unprotected edge of his booth.

"Head for Wheels," Jonah said, indicating the biker bar down by the wharf. "It's the closest cover."

The four of them took off running, leaving the lit area of the carnival behind and heading toward the wharf as the rain grew harder. They cut over to Waterfront Avenue by dashing down the street between the ice cream parlor and the fortune-telling stand, both of which had closed for the evening.

A gust of wind coming off of Raven's Cove blew rain into Becca's face and whipped her clothes against her body before they finally reached the overhang in front of Wheels. They stomped the mud from their shoes and pushed through the door of the bar to a loud twanging of guitar music from the aging jukebox.

"Tables are all taken," a buxom blond waitress said as she sashayed by them, "but there's room at the bar."

"The bar's fine with me," Jonah said, "as long as the beer's cold. How about you ladies?"

"I can handle that," Becca said.

"I've been known to straddle a stool," Kat agreed, slipping out of her wet jacket and tossing it over a hook by the door. The others followed suit as a couple of guys moved over to give them four seats together. Becca and Kat took the inside seats so they could talk to each other over the music and loud voices.

The middle-aged bartender wiped his hands on a stained apron and leaned over the counter. "Looks like you got caught in the rain. You must have been at the carnival."

"Yeah," Jonah answered. "Poor planning on our part, Jake. If we'd started at the far end and worked our way back, we'd have been at the car by the time the rain hit. As it was, we were at the end by the wharf.''

"Well, at least you got to see it all. Not that it changes much from year to year. What'll it be?''

They gave him their orders, and Becca and Larry showed their IDs. Jonah and Kat didn't bother. Jonah's cousin had owned the bar across the street before he died, and both Jonah and Kat had been in Wheels often enough that the bartender knew they were legal age.

Becca propped her booted feet on the foot rail and let her gaze scan the dim bar while Larry excused himself to go to the men's room.

The wharf area always intrigued her. The environment stripped away pretense and social niceties. What you saw was what you got, and no one bothered to mince words just to spare someone's feelings. Like the two men who were sitting a few seats down from them. She wasn't eavesdropping, but their gruff voices carried easily.

"I'm not afraid of no damn ghost. Not after what I face day in and day out. I say if that Leary fellow rises from his grave, put him on a fishing boat and send him out into a raging storm. One giant wave, and the man will go running back to his safe spot six feet under.''

"Well, someone killed that girl. Matt Jackson was the first cop on the scene and his old lady told mine it was as gory a sight he'd ever seen. Blood everywhere. Hardly had a drop left in her.''

A guy in faded jeans and a worn leather jacket banged his fork on the table. "Would you guys keep it down? Some people are trying to eat in here.''

Kat waited until the bartender set the beers in front of them. "What is this about a murder?''

He leaned in close. "A young woman, late teens or

early twenties. Some boys out on their mud bikes found the body in the bushes off of Old Mountain Road just before dark. The police are trying to keep a lid on it until they find out more about it, but you can't keep anything quiet around this town. You know that.''

''Did they identify her?''

''Not as far as I know. She'd been dead awhile. That's all I heard.''

Becca felt herself getting sick and wished she hadn't eaten the chili-soaked hot dog at the carnival.

The man two seats down from Becca broke into the conversation. ''It's that Bryson fellow that done it.''

''You shouldn't say things like that when you have no proof,'' Kat warned.

''I got all the proof I need. The man sits up there in his castle all day, supposedly brooding over some lost lover. Then he comes snooping around town at night. I've seen him plenty of times. If he wasn't up to no good, he'd show himself in the daytime like a real man. He did it. I'd bet my Harley on it.''

Jake slid a foamy beer toward him. ''Your Harley? Put up a night with your woman, and I'll take your bet.''

''Marie wouldn't have you, you beer-splattered buzzard.'' He took a long drag on his beer. ''So are you on the side of the beast?''

''I'm not on anyone's side,'' Jake answered, ''but I don't think the man's dangerous. He's just a little addled, that's all. You'd be, too, if you lost your fiancée the way he did.''

''Humph!'' The second man slapped a beefy hand on the counter. ''I say he was the one who murdered Tasha Pierce. She went up to that haunted house of his to break up with him, and he killed her. Almost killed himself in the process.''

"He's crazy, all right," the first man added. "Should be locked up in that same hospital where they put that poor Cavendish girl when she was kidnapped from the graveyard."

The words ground into Becca's mind, and David Bryson's face appeared in front of her, so real she felt she could reach out and touch it. The beer almost slipped from her hands as she set it back on the bar.

"This talk is getting to you, isn't it?" Kat said, turning her attention to Becca. "You're shaking, and perspiration is popping out on your forehead."

"It's the smoke and the stale air," she lied. "I think I'll step out the door and get a breath of air."

"You'll get wet."

"I'll stay under the overhang," Becca assured her, already climbing down from the barstool.

"I'll go with you."

"No. Please. Stay and visit with Jonah. I'll be just outside the door."

Kat touched her arm. "I'll be right here if you need me."

"Thanks, but I'll be fine." She walked away, yanked her jacket from the hook and pushed through the door. Once outside, she leaned against the side of the building for support. The rain had slowed to a drizzle, but the wind howled around the corners and cut through her light windbreaker.

Only the real chill came from somewhere deep inside her. She'd had the crazy feeling all day that something terrible was going to happen. Now she found out a young woman's body had been found off the road leading up to the Bluffs.

But how did she know? Why? She buried her hands deep in the pockets of her jacket.

"Rebecca Smith."

Her heart jumped to her throat at the sound of her name. She spun around and stared at a figure, half hidden in the shadows of the old clapboard building. He stepped toward her. Her knees grew weak and rubbery and she stood frozen to the cement beneath her feet.

Escape would probably be impossible, anyway. The beast from the Bluffs had come for *her*.

Chapter Two

The voice was hypnotic, almost haunting and emotions thick as chowder churned inside Becca. "What do you want?" she whispered, her throat so dry, she could barely form the words.

"I didn't mean to frighten you," he said, stepping closer.

She stared at him but only saw his profile. He kept his face turned toward the street. "You don't frighten me. I was only startled because I didn't realize you were out there."

"Then I apologize for not making more noise on my approach."

"Why don't you look at me when you talk?"

"I have my reasons."

"If it's to save me from the sight of your face, you needn't bother, Dr. Bryson. I'm sure I can handle it."

"So you know who I am?"

"Of course. Everyone does." And they'd all tremble in terror if they knew she was alone with him on a dark, deserted street. Yet the strange feelings coursing through her senses right now lacked the stringent sting of fear she'd felt when he'd first called her name. She pulled her windbreaker tighter. "What do you want from me?"

"Professional services."

"In what way?"

"My house, the Bluffs. Do you know it?"

"I've only seen it from a distance. It appears more a castle than a house."

"A dark castle."

"I still don't understand, Dr. Bryson. What does your dark castle have to do with me?"

"I'd like for you to change it. Let in the light. You know, add color."

"Are you looking for someone to redecorate the Bluffs?"

"Yes." He exhaled sharply, as if her saying the words gave him some kind of release. "Can you do that?"

"I'm merely a seamstress, not an interior designer."

"But you do sometimes sew drapes and slipcovers?"

"Occasionally."

"Then I'd like to hire you."

His voice seemed to reach inside her and awake some unexplainable eros, which defied reason. Fear edged along her nerve endings now, but she had no idea if it was due to the doctor's presence or to her own bizarre reaction to him. "I'm not the person you need."

He drew away and put his hand to his face as if to shield her from the infamous scar that was already hidden from her line of vision. "You won't have to see me," he said. "I'll stay in my lab while you work and you can correspond with me through my butler, Richard Crawford."

"It's not that."

"Then what is it? I'll pay you well."

"I'm sorry. I just can't do it."

He shuffled and stuck his hands deep into the front

pockets of his trousers. "I understand. I'm sorry I bothered you. I promise I won't do it again."

Hurt seeped into his voice. She recognized the sound of it but had never expected to hear it coming from his mouth. It humanized him in a way nothing else could have and made her wonder at her own heartlessness.

The door opened behind her and Larry stepped through it. "Kat said you were feeling a little nauseous. Do you want me to borrow Jake's car and..." He stopped midsentence as his gaze took in the shadowy profile of David Bryson. His hands knotted into fists, and he stepped between the two of them as if blocking her from some type of attack. "What are you doing here?" he demanded. "Frightening defenseless women?"

David's muscles tensed. "Something like that," he said. "But don't worry, I'm leaving now."

"Yes." The word flew from her mouth. She didn't know why or when she'd changed her mind. "I accept your offer."

David stopped in his tracks. "Are you certain?"

She nodded. "I'll come out to your place tomorrow if that's convenient."

"Tomorrow will be fine. I'll send Richard for you. Would ten be too early?"

"No. He can pick me up at the shop."

Larry clamped his hand around her arm as David disappeared into the shadows. "What are you talking about? Are you crazy?"

Crazy? The term seemed fitting, but she wasn't going to stand outside and argue with him about it. She owed him no explanation. It wasn't as if they were more than casual friends. "This doesn't concern you."

"Maybe not, but you can't be serious about going to the Bluffs. What did he tell you? Did he threaten you?"

"No." She pulled the door open and marched back inside the bar with Larry at her heels. She had an idea that it was going to be a long, long night.

BECCA STRETCHED BETWEEN the cool sheets and stared out the window near her bed. The rain had stopped, and the clouds moved across the night sky like black sheets being tossed by the wind. She never felt truly at home, but she usually felt safe and protected in her small, rented nook inside the Cavendish home. Tonight even the familiar surroundings seemed eerily foreign.

Kat and Jonah hadn't agreed with Larry's assessment that she was crazy, but even they had warned her to be cautious. A lot of people in town didn't trust Dr. Bryson. The superstitious rumors of ghosts and warlocks aside, the man was antisocial and decidedly weird. Some even thought he was a killer.

She had no argument for them. If someone had suggested before tonight that she'd be paying Dr. David Bryson a visit tomorrow, she'd have thought them nuts. But there was no denying that she wanted to see him again. She'd liked his voice, or perhaps been mesmerized by it would be the more apt description. Rich, but with a hint of sadness and a whisper of heartbreak.

Hints and whispers. Egads! Now she was beginning to sound like one of the guides giving a practiced spiel to paying tourists. The simple, unadorned truth was that the man was a recluse who dressed in black and only came out of his fortress at night. And she had agreed to go to his castle like some poor sheep being led to slaughter.

The only thing to do was call the man in the morning and back out. Rolling over, she pounded her fists into the pillow before plopping her head back in the middle of it. All she had to say was that she'd changed her mind. What could he do but take no for an answer?

The wind whistled around the corner of the house, and she tugged the covers up to her neck and closed her eyes. "Sorry, Dr. Bryson. I'm not coming," she whispered.

"Please, I need you, Becca."

The words slammed into her senses, and her heart thundered in her chest. Opening her eyes wide, she jerked to a sitting position. The room was empty. The voice had been only her imagination working overtime. She lay on her back and stared at the ceiling, wishing she'd never gone to the carnival and never run into David Bryson. Perhaps it would have been better if she'd never moved to Moriah's Landing at all.

A town with a history of witch trials and hangings on the town green. A town haunted by ghosts and abductions and unsolved murders. Yet, from the very first day she'd visited Moriah's Landing, she'd felt as if she belonged here. And she desperately needed to belong somewhere.

Thunder crashed and lightning zigzagged in a blinding display of electric current, and the rain started up again. She closed her eyes and tried to concentrate on the screaming wind and the sound of rain pelting against the windows. Instead, the voice of David Bryson haunted her mind. Smooth, mysterious, seductive.

The storm had passed and the first rays of the sun were already peeking over the horizon before she finally fell asleep. By then she knew that she'd have to make tomorrow's visit to the Bluffs, if only to satisfy her own curiosity and convince herself that Dr. David Bryson was just a man with no power over her. She would not lose another night's sleep over him.

CLAIRE CAVENDISH HURRIED down the narrow streets, dodging puddles left from last night's deluge. Foreboding pooled inside her, much like the water that gathered in the cracks and crevices of the cobbled street. She couldn't imagine what Becca was thinking, but she knew she had to stop her.

She had liked Becca from the moment she met her, already knew all about her from Elizabeth, Brie and Kat, three of Claire's closest friends.

It wasn't unusual that Becca had become part of the same circle of friends that Claire had shared all her life. Once Becca and Elizabeth had become friends, it was only natural that Elizabeth would introduce her to the others. Now they were all friends, and Claire would not stand by and watch while Becca made a horrible mistake.

Becca had no way of knowing the things that Claire knew. She couldn't know how Dr. David Bryson had bewitched her friend Tasha Pierce, lured her into his life and led her to her death. Claire pictured Tasha as she'd been then. Vivacious, innocent, drunk on life. Both of them had been so excited over beginning their first year at Heathrow College.

Within a month of starting at Heathrow, the hopes and dreams vanished for both of them. Tasha had died. Claire had lived, at least that's what the psychiatrists had kept reminding her. All she knew know was that she would not stand by and watch Becca fall into the same trap she'd stepped into during sorority rush week five years ago. A lifetime ago. Stepped into that dark mausoleum.

Stepped into hell.

Apprehension churned in her stomach. Becca would have to listen to her. She'd make her. The Bluffs was not the same as a mausoleum, but it could prove just as dangerous.

BECCA FILLED TWO MUGS with fresh perked coffee from the large pot in Threads and handed one to Claire. Claire's hands shook as she took the cup, and Becca's heart went out to her. She'd been through so much. Still, she'd been steadily improving over the last few weeks and months, and Becca hated to see her as upset as she was right now.

She reached out and laid a hand on Claire's shoulder. "If you're having a bad day, it might help to talk about it."

Claire wrapped both hands around her cup. "I talked to Larry Gayle this morning."

If Larry had been available right now, Becca would have gladly wrung his neck. "He shouldn't have called you, Claire. Everything's fine."

"He didn't call. Mother's old Ford was sounding funny and she asked him to take a look at it. He's good with cars, and planned to become a mechanic before he went to work in his dad's hardware store. We talked while he was there and he told me about last night."

"Larry Gayle talks too much."

"You can't go to the Bluffs, Becca. You can't work for that—that *beast*."

"Oh, Claire, he's not a beast. He's just a recluse, and if anyone here had reason to become one, it's him. And he certainly can't help the fact that he's scarred. You surely don't hold that against him."

"No. This isn't about the way he looks." Claire set her coffee cup on the table and walked to the window. She stared through it for long, pregnant seconds before turning back to Becca. "You're new in town, Becca.

You weren't here five years ago when the evil erupted. You didn't know Tasha, how beautiful she was, how sweet.''

"I've heard you and her other friends speak of her. I know she must have been a very special person."

"She was. And then David Bryson came into her life. He used his powers to seduce her—mentally, physically, spiritually. He was all she could talk about, all she thought about."

"They were in love. It's like that when you're in love, or so I've heard." She spoke tenderly, trying to ease the pain and fear that still claimed so much of Claire.

"Tasha was too young to be in love, especially with a man like David Bryson. She was naive and innocent, only eighteen. He was thirty-five, polished, sophisticated. But he was a fake. He'd grown up right here in Moriah's Landing, the son of a woman who sold her body for men to—well, you know…"

"If you're saying his mother was a prostitute, I'm sure he had no control over that."

"It wasn't just his mother. David was a hotheaded kid who was always in trouble. My mother remembers him, and so does everyone else in this town who's over forty."

"People change, Claire. David Bryson changed. He's become a doctor. There's no reason to think he's anything like he was as a teenager."

"Then how do you explain how he got the money to buy the Bluffs?"

"I'm guessing he earned it."

Claire turned from the window and stared at Becca. Her long blond hair hung around her sunken cheeks and her blue eyes appeared haunted. That, combined with the paleness of her skin and her slim build, made her appear like an abandoned child much younger than her twenty-three years. She placed both hands on the cutting table and leaned forward.

"Please, Becca, even if you think David Bryson is harmless, stay away from him. A lot of people in this town believe he murdered Tasha."

"I asked Kat about that when I first heard about him. She said there was never any real evidence against him and that eventually the explosion that killed Tasha was ruled an accident."

"Only because they couldn't find any evidence that it was a planted explosion, but the Pierces don't think he's innocent."

"Oh, Claire, honey, the Pierces lost a member of their family. You can't expect them to be objective about all of this. But from what I can tell, Dr. Bryson is just a man who's had a very difficult life."

"He's not what he seems, Becca. Whatever he wants from you, it has nothing to do with redecorating his house."

Claire's voice trembled and Becca's heart went out to her. She knew the story of how Claire had gone with Tasha, Kat, Brie and Elizabeth to the cemetery as part of a sorority initiation. The one who drew the piece of paper with the picture of McFarland Leary on it had to go into the haunted mausoleum. That had been Claire. While inside, she'd been abducted, and whatever had happened to her while she was in the hands of the madman had left her a shattered shell of the young woman she'd been.

It was no wonder she was so afraid of a mysterious man like David. But Becca had to make her own decisions this time, and she couldn't base them on groundless fear. "I'm sure the Bluffs can use a little updating," she said, keeping her tone light. "I have no reason to think that's not the reason he came to me."

"But why *you*, Becca? With his money he can hire a professional from Boston to come out and redecorate the Bluffs or hire one of the local interior designers. Why would he seek out a young seamstress without any experience in interior design? And why would he come to you in the dark of night instead of during shop hours?"

The questions Claire asked were all valid. Becca couldn't deny that. The man could afford to hire anyone he wanted and yet he'd come to her. "I appreciate your concern, but…"

"But you're not backing out of the job."

Becca stared into her coffee cup, hating to meet Claire's worried gaze. "I can't, not yet, anyway."

"See, he's already gotten to you."

Becca looked up. It was straight up ten o'clock, and a tall, neatly dressed gentleman was headed up the walk. She couldn't deny feeling anxious and uneasy, but she also knew that she was going with David's butler. She walked over and gave her friend a comforting hug. "I have to go now, Claire, but I'll be home early tonight. Why don't the two of us go for dinner at the Beachway Diner? I'll tell you all about my visit to the Bluffs and you'll see that I'm fine."

Claire turned to the door. "It's not too late to change your mind."

Becca shook her head. "Dinner at seven." She forced a smile as she escorted Claire to the door. "I'll meet you at the diner, and don't worry. Who's afraid of the big, bad beast?"

"Me," Claire said, but she squeezed Becca's hand as she opened the door and stepped around the imposing man without even looking at him.

Becca held the door open. "I'm Becca Smith, and you must be Richard Crawford."

"Yes. Are you ready for me to drive you to the Bluffs?"

"As soon as I lock up and put the Be Back Later sign on the door." Luckily the owner gave her permission to set her own hours.

"There's no hurry, but if I can be of assistance, just let me know," Richard offered.

"That's okay. I have everything under control." She picked up a large sketch pad and a couple of sharpened pencils and dropped them into a canvas tote bag that already held her tape measure and a calculator.

Who's afraid of the big, bad beast? The chant echoed in her head as she hung the sign over the hook on the door. In approximately half an hour, she'd step inside the massive stone castle on the top of the highest cliff in this part of the state, a structure that no one she knew had set foot in for the last five years. Hidden away from the city, in a world of secrets guarded by a stone fence and an electric gate. Just she and Richard and Dr. David Bryson.

Who was afraid now that the time had come?

She was. That's who.

FROM A DISTANCE, the Bluffs was impressive and imposing. Up close and personal it was downright formidable. The stone was dark gray, scarred by centuries of gale-force winds, driving rains and the burning heat of summer. The curves and angles of the structure stretched out in all directions, large enough to house a small army, with turrets and parapets along the roof line and hideous gargoyles and ferocious creatures from some imaginary animal kingdom posed as silent, ominous guards over it all.

"Don't let the size intimidate you," Richard offered as they stepped to the massive wooden door. "It's basically just a house."

Yeah, and the Taj Mahal was just a tomb. Anxiety and anticipation warred inside her as Richard fitted a large metal key into the lock and turned it. This would be her first look inside the edifice that had fascinated her from her first glimpse of it. Her first step inside the bastion of a man half the town thought was a blood-sucking vampire and the other half believed was a murderer.

Her heart hammered against her chest as the heavy door creaked open. Claire's warning crept into her mind, but she pushed it aside. If she'd been afraid to face the new and unfamiliar, she'd have died years ago.

"This is it," Richard said as he followed her inside. "Welcome to the home of Dr. David Bryson."

"Wow." Juvenile comment, but she was lucky to have gotten that out. "It's so...I mean, it's awesome." She turned, her gaze jumping from the magnificent ceilings to the Victorian chandeliers, from the beautiful but worn Persian rugs to the exquisite antique furnishings. Dark, dreary colors, and yet the sheer grandeur was enough to take her breath away. She walked over and stopped in front of the massive marble fireplace. "I've never seen anything like it. I didn't even know places like this existed outside of fairy tales."

"I know exactly how you feel. I felt that way myself the first time I came here to interview for the position of Dr. Bryson's butler."

She doubted that. Richard Crawford had been nice and friendly enough on the drive up to the Bluffs, but he was far too sophisticated for her to ever imagine him all but drooling over a house the way she was. She needed to get a grip, make herself sound more professional. "The house and furnishings are quite resplendent, but I must agree with the doctor's assessment that the place needs updating." Resplendent? She sounded more like some society snob than a professional. "New window treatments and more colorful coverings for the furniture would make the place much brighter and more livable," she added, trying to salvage a shred of credibility out of the conversation.

"I agree wholeheartedly. I've mentioned it many times over the last few years, but David, Dr. Bryson that is, never seemed interested until now."

"And are you and Dr. Bryson the only ones who live here?"

"It's just the two of us, though there are others who work here during the day. There's a cook and a small staff of gardeners and housekeepers. None of them are here today, though. Saturdays and Sundays are typically the days off for all the staff."

"When is your day off?"

"Whenever I need one. Are you ready for me to show you around?"

So David was planning to keep the promise he made last night, stay out of sight and leave her in the hands of Richard. She should be thankful. She wasn't. Now that she'd seen where he lived, she was even more intrigued by him. Besides, unless she talked to him face-to-face, dealt with him as a real flesh-and-blood person, she might never banish him from her thoughts and fantasies or stop hearing his mesmerizing voice echo in her mind. "I would prefer to do the walk-through with the owner."

"I'm sorry, but he gave specific instructions that I was

to deal with you myself. Of course, I'll take all your ideas to him and he will be the one to make any final decisions on what is to be changed.''

"Then we may as well get started. Since only two of you live here and it doesn't appear that your employer does much entertaining, you can't possibly use all the rooms.''

"No, there're over seventy of them, not counting the lab in the west wing.''

Seventy rooms. It baffled the mind, but she had no trouble believing that it was true. She surveyed the room they were in. New drapes were definitely needed. The ones hanging were streaked and faded and so thick they blocked every trace of sunlight from the room. The chairs should be recovered, too, in something soft and welcoming. And the room needed lamps, low wattage, to throw halos of light where it was needed.

And that was in just one room. If she took this job, it would take her months to even begin to make a showing, especially if she had to fit it in between her regular sewing jobs.

"Could I get you something to drink before we get started?'' Richard asked.

"No, and to tell you the truth, Mr. Crawford, I'm not at all sure I can handle this job.''

"I'm sure Dr. Bryson didn't contact you about this without checking into your credentials first.''

"My credentials are that I design and sew dresses for local ladies who want something a little different from what they can buy off the rack in a department store. I'm good at that, and I work at reasonable rates. Now, if there's any way David Bryson can stretch that into proper qualifications for this job, I certainly don't see it.''

She walked to the cluster of windows that covered the entire back wall and tugged the heavy drape to the side. The breath rushed from her lungs as she took in the view. This room overlooked the cliff, looked down on the swirling blue water that splashed against the jagged rocks of Raven's Cove.

She spotted a man kneeling on the edge of the cliff, a beautiful bouquet of pure white roses in his hand. He scattered them over the rocks and then stood, staring at the water far below. It wasn't until he turned back toward the house that she recognized him. Her breath caught unexpectedly.

"I see your boss now. Why is he laying roses out to dry?"

"He's not. He lost his fiancée to those waters below us. The roses are his way of honoring her memory."

"But that was years ago."

"It's a tradition he's kept up over the years."

"You know, Richard, since he's the one who'll be paying me if I take this job, I think I'll just go and discuss the redecorating project with him."

"That is not a good idea."

"Why not? He's obviously not working."

"His wishes are that you deal with me."

"I don't work that way."

He motioned to his left. "There's a back exit just down that hall, but I'm warning you that Dr. Bryson will not be happy to see you."

Fine. She hadn't been that happy to see him in the shadows last night, either, but he'd looked her up all the same. Credentials be hanged. She had none and she was beginning to agree with Claire. Whatever David Bryson wanted from her, it probably had nothing to do with redecorating his house. There was no time like the present to find out for certain.

She started down the hall.

Richard followed her. "You're making a mistake."

"It won't be my first and hopefully not my last." Strange, but she could have sworn Richard was smiling when she caught that last glimpse of him as she headed out the door for a meeting with Moriah Landing's most infamous mad scientist.

Mad, maybe. But a man who strew flowers in honor of a fiancée who'd been dead for five years couldn't be all bad. At least she hoped that was true, because he'd spotted her coming toward him now and he'd ducked into a small stone structure that sat precipitously close to the edge of the cliff. And she was about to join him.

Chapter Three

David let the last of the roses slip from his hands and onto the potting table as he watched Rebecca Smith walk down the cobbled path, her hips swaying in a full cotton skirt that swished around her calves. Hair the color of cornsilk bounced along the collar of a tailored white blouse, and a soft heather cardigan was tied around her narrow shoulders. Feminine, with an understated sexuality that clung like an invisible but intoxicating aura.

Old feelings stirred inside him, and his hands grew clammy. He took one step backward, suddenly painfully aware of his limp and the jagged edges of the scar that ran its freakish path down his face. Picking up a clay pot half filled with dirt, he added water and splattered the muddy concoction over the one window, all but blocking the sunlight from the back of the small, angular structure.

He'd been a fool to seek Becca out and invite her into his world—a fool to bring any woman into his life. Had he not been outwardly disfigured, he'd still have nothing to offer. The unseen scars that cut a barbed swath clear across his heart and soul had proved to be the most destructive wounds of all.

She paused at the door, staring tentatively inside.

He stayed in the back shadows but turned to the right in an attempt to shield her as much as possible from the disgusting sight of the damaged side of his face. "Is there something I can do for you, Miss Smith?"

"Please, call me Becca. Everyone does. And, yes, there is something you can do."

"If it's about the house, Richard has the authority to make any decisions necessary based on what you tell him. I trust your judgment."

"To be quite honest with you, Dr. Bryson, I'm not certain my judgment is worth much in this situation."

"I'm sure you underestimate your ability."

"No. If you want a party dress, I'm your woman. I've even made drapes and slipcovers before, but I've always done it according to the wishes of the owner or a professional decorator. I've never taken on an entire remodeling job on my own."

Her manner of speaking caught him off guard. He'd expected her to be softer, more reticent. A big mistake on his part. She was forthright and spunky as hell. "Are you refusing my offer, Becca?"

"That's not what I said."

"Then I don't see a problem. I trust you, and Richard is authorized to handle this project. I will meet with you from time to time, but in the future, I will choose the time and the place." He was coming on too strong. If he wasn't careful, he'd frighten her away, and now that he was so close to her, he wanted her here at the Bluffs even more than he'd wanted her before.

And knowing that filled him with a choking wave of guilt that defied all reason. Guilt and the knowledge that having her on the premises was a dreadful mistake. And still he wanted her.

ANGER SURFACED, SWELLED, shook Becca to the core. The man had some nerve, but she would not be treated like a second-rate servant of his, dismissed with a nod of his head. "I haven't agreed to take this job yet, but I won't even consider tackling it without your full cooperation."

He turned the left side of his face toward her and met her gaze. His eyes were dark, piercing, totally unnerving. "Exactly what do you mean by my cooperation?"

"I'd like for you to walk with me through the rooms that you'd like updated. You can tell me what colors you like, what style you prefer, the function of each room in your everyday life."

"You want me to walk with you?" He made it sound like an incredible request, as if she'd asked him to sleep with her or father her unborn children.

"Walk and talk, Dr. Bryson. It's really not all that difficult. I'm an intelligent and quite charming woman, once you get to know me."

"Your intelligence was never in question."

"If this is because of your face, I can assure you that your staying in the shadows is not necessary."

His eyes grew hard, the muscles in his face rigid. "How I handle my deformity is actually none of your concern."

Poor guy. Had Moriah's Landing done that to him, made him think of himself as a monster? Or did the feeling come from something far deeper than his physical wounds? When she spoke again, her voice was little more than a whisper. "A man is more than the way he looks."

"True. And you must trust me the way I trust you. I want you to do the work at the Bluffs, but I can only deal with you on my terms. You will be safe here, and I will pay you whatever you ask.''

''Even if the amount is unreasonable?''

''It won't be.''

''How do you know?

''Because I know you, Becca.''

His voice crawled inside her, then spread through her like fingers of fire. She could turn and walk away right now, never come to this place again, never see David again. But even if she did, she knew she'd still hear his voice at night. He'd still stalk the corners of her consciousness. The only way she would ever get over him would be to get to know him, to realize he was just a man and that he held no paranormal powers over her.

Besides, the job would pay well, help her start saving money so that she could eventually buy Threads. It would also keep her busy over the long winter months when other work would be scarce. Once the Fall Extravaganza and the Christmas ball were over, life in Moriah's Landing would settle back into the routine of daily living, and the need for party dresses would come to an abrupt end.

The decision-making was over. She would take the job. David Bryson was not your average citizen of Moriah's Landing, but then neither was she.

''I'll take the job,'' she said.

''I'm glad.''

And that was it. A few seconds later, she turned, left the stone gardening building and started back to the house. Alone.

THE BEACHWAY DINER WAS noisy and filled with the odors of grease, onions and fishermen in nubby, worn sweaters and rubber boots. Not the classiest spot in town, but the food was always good. Shamus McManus sat at a back table, only half listening to the ranting of Marley Glasglow and Kevin Pinelle. His cod sandwich and bowl of chowder would have gone down a lot easier in better company than either one of them, but when the diner was this crowded, a man had to share with whoever needed a seat.

Marley had lived in Moriah's Landing all his life—probably close to thirty-five years. He didn't do any kind of work too regularly, but he hired on with a boat captain often enough to keep his beer belly and his sour disposition. Shamus was sixty-eight, and he'd seen Marley grow more surly and disagreeable with every passing year. This one was no exception.

Kevin was a young fly-by-night, who was working the boats for the summer, signing up with first one fisherman and then another. He was way too sociable for Shamus's taste, hung out in the wharf bars every night he wasn't out on a boat, usually with some sweet, young looker on his arm. Obviously, the women went for his physique and boyish charm. Of course, if one of them showed up pregnant and claiming he was the father, he'd probably be out of town before the sun set.

"I think we should march up to the Bluffs and tell that murderer to keep his hands off our women," Marley said, talking with his mouth full—a thoroughly disgusting sight.

"I didn't know you had any women," Kevin joked. "The way you complain about the fairer sex, I'm surprised you're not glad to let Bryson or the ghost of Leary have his pick."

Marley sneered and stuffed a few more French fries into his mouth. "I like them fine. Wouldn't trust one as far as I can spit, but they're all right in their place."

"Yeah," Kevin said. "I feel the same way, except I'll take them in their place or mine."

"I just don't get it," Marley continued, this time swallowing first. "Why would a good-looking woman like that seamstress go up to the Bluffs to see a dangerous lunatic? Unless she's a descendant of one of the Moriah's Landing witches and is going up there to consort with her own kind."

Shamus shook his head and pushed his plate away. He'd had his fill of the sandwich and Marley. "Becca Smith's no witch and you damned well know it. And if it was any of your business what she was doing at the Bluffs, she'd have told you."

Kevin propped his elbows on the table. "Yeah, but as much as I hate to admit it, Marley might actually have a valid point this time. Bryson is weird, acts like some freaking vampire, never coming out except at night. And I saw him talking to Becca outside Wheels last night."

"A freaking vampire. That's him, all right. So why would a beautiful woman let herself get picked up in the man's own car and driven to his godforsaken castle?"

"Do you know for a fact that she did?" Shamus asked.

Marley leaned forward. "I saw her with my own eyes. I was just leaving the liquor store when I saw her get in the car with Bryson's butler. I followed them all the way to the road for the Bluffs."

"Maybe Bryson's trying to get to Claire Cavendish through Becca," Kevin offered. "That would make sense if he's the one who kidnapped Claire in the first place, and a lot of folks think he is."

Shamus plucked his fishing hat from the back of his chair. "That's hogwash."

"Yeah, but if he did kidnap Claire, he might be afraid

she's going to remember enough to get him arrested now that she's out of the hospital,'' Kevin argued. ''Becca does live in the Cavendish house, you know. And the two of them are friends. I've seen them out together.''

''It would be just like the guy,'' Marley said, his face growing red and his voice lowering to a husky whisper. ''The dirty, murdering son of a bitch. We've had enough of David Bryson in this town. It's time somebody around here gets rid of him once and for all.''

Shamus stared him down. ''Someone might one day, but it won't be you. You're a dirty coward to the bone, Marley Glasglow. All bark and not enough teeth left in your ugly mouth to bite.''

''Go to hell.''

''I probably will. I'm just hoping it's not today.'' Shamus pulled a few wrinkled bills from his front pocket and dropped enough money on the table to cover his tab and a small tip.

A few seconds later, he stepped out the door, the news about Becca Smith visiting David Bryson hitting him like a bottle of cheap wine. But unlike Kevin and Marley, he had enough sense to keep his opinions to himself.

IT WAS FIFTEEN MINUTES past three o'clock when Becca thanked Richard for the ride home and climbed out of David's black sedan. The partial tour of the house had lasted until one-thirty. After that, she had eaten the lunch Richard had served, a cream-based soup, a green salad and a chicken-pasta dish as good as any she'd ever eaten. He'd said the accolades belonged to the cook, who was off today.

Richard had joined her for lunch, and they'd talked at length about possibilities for the house. Once she'd taken the tour, ideas had leapt into her mind at the speed of light, and she'd worried that she sounded more like a kid with a new toy than a professional with a new challenge. It seemed that money would not be an object and that both David and Richard trusted her judgment implicitly. The only restriction was that she limit her work to the bottom floor of the east wing of the house.

Reaching into the deep pockets of her skirt, she pulled out the key and fit it into the lock. A white envelope was taped to the door just above the knob. Apparently one of her customers had dropped by while she was out, though she always encouraged them to call first. She pulled the note from the door and stuffed it into the canvas tote.

The familiarity of the shop wrapped around her as she stepped inside and switched on the light. Although she only managed Threads, the owner seldom took any interest in the place anymore. That worked out well for Becca. In a lot of ways the shop was more home to her than her room in the Cavendish house. At work, her mind stayed busy, found creative outlets for the restlessness and waves of undefinable anxiety that never fully deserted her. But alone at night, there was no escaping the fact that no matter how hard she pretended otherwise, Becca Smith was a total fraud.

She started a pot of fresh coffee, then retrieved the envelope that had been taped to her door. Fitting the tip of a silver letter opener beneath the seal, she ripped the envelope and slipped the note out and into the light. It was written on lined notebook paper, with black magic marker, the print crude and uneven.

Stay away from David Bryson or risk meeting the same fate as Natasha Pierce.

The print was childlike. The message was not. She read the note out loud, then shook her head as the initial

wave of anxiety settled into disgust. If this was someone's idea of a joke, it wasn't funny. But more likely it
was a genuine warning from one of the locals who had
been exposed to the tales of witchcraft and murderous
mad scientists for so long, they actually believed them.

She kept busy as the coffee finished perking, putting
away her samples, straightening a stack of fabrics, wa-
tering her potted ivy. When the coffee was ready, she
poured a cup and dropped to her sewing chair.

Images of the Bluffs crowded her mind. The place was
magnificent. It was difficult to believe that someone in
the seventeenth century had the vision or the money to
build such an incredible structure.

For the first time in—in as long as she could remember—she had found a project she could sink her teeth
into. She would bring the Bluffs back to life, and just
maybe she'd bring its strange owner back to life, as well.
If she did, some woman would thank her for it.

Unless… She picked up the note and stared at it again.
Unless David Bryson really wasn't the man he seemed.
Unless he really was the man who had killed those
women twenty years ago. Unless he was the man who
had kidnapped and tortured poor Claire Cavendish until
he'd driven her out of her mind.

She tried to picture him in that role. The image didn't
jell. Still, she'd make better decisions if she relied on
facts instead of rumors and groundless superstitions. She
usually kept the shop open on Saturday for the benefit
of customers who worked during the week, but she'd
already been out of the shop for hours so a couple more
wouldn't matter.

And right now sitting at the sewing machine didn't
seem nearly as urgent as going to the library to peruse
the microfilm file of newspapers from twenty years ago.

She knew they were there—just one more of the famous tourist draws to a town that made a lucrative business out of fear and superstition. But Moriah's Landing didn't have the monopoly on that. Everyone believed what they wanted.

In the end, she probably would, too.

FOURTH YOUNG WOMAN This Year Found Murdered.

Becca shivered and crossed her arms over her chest as she read the sketchy but chilling account of the murder. Apparently, few facts had been released to the paper, but she'd heard bizarre tales about the gruesome side of the killings from several of her customers. The events had occurred twenty years ago, but sitting alone in the library, immersed in the newspaper articles, she had the eerie feeling that the bodies were still as fresh as the one that had just been found on Old Mountain Road, not far from the Bluffs.

The first murder had been solved. The last three had not. The fourth victim had been Joyce Telatia, of the Boston Telatias, one of the wealthiest families in the Northeast. The killer could have probably made millions in ransom if he'd only kidnapped her and not killed her. But apparently it was death and not money that drove the monster. And his lust for murder might well have been fueled by publicity surrounding the vicious murder of Leslie Ridgemont, Kat's mother. In that case the motive had been jealousy and lust, but with the three later victims, there appeared to be no motive, just random killings of innocent victims.

Becca blinked and tried to clear her eyes, but a couple of salty tears mingled with her fatigue, and she pushed away from the viewer. She'd had all she could take for one day. She glanced at her watch. If she hurried, she'd have enough time to locate and check out a couple of books that had been written on the history of witchcraft in Moriah's Landing before she met Claire for dinner.

Bedtime reading sure to produce nightmares. So much for sleep.

THE AFTERNOON IN THE LAB had been totally unproductive, and David had given up on his current experiment after a couple of hours. He'd taken the secret passage that led from the library to an ancient world of darkness, always wondering when he did why he frequently found that world of black chambers studded with skulls and bones more welcoming than the one he lived in.

He'd stayed there the rest of the afternoon, perusing the mountain of meticulously kept notes that had once belonged to Dr. Leland Manning. Dr. Manning had been the major influencing factor in David's decision to go into medical research. Now the man was in prison for conducting illegal and unethical experiments in genetic engineering. It seemed there was no explaining how far a man could go once he passed the line from reason to madness.

David exited the secret door and closed it behind him, leaving only a wall of bookcases where the opening had been. He crossed the library and started down the long hallway, the echoes of his footsteps a lonesome sound that always reminded him how different it would have been in the Bluffs had Tasha lived. He stopped at the door to the bedroom they would have shared.

Reaching into his pocket, he took out the key ring and fit the key into the lock, then hesitated as thoughts of Becca haunted his mind. So different from Tasha. Far less innocent. Spunky, instead. Determined. Direct. Full, rounded breasts. Sensuous, swaying hips.

His throat constricted, and he dropped his hand from the door. The room belonged to the past, to a love as pure as the white roses he scattered on the cliffs every week, and he wouldn't defile it with the thoughts running roughshod through his mind now.

He hurried down the hall and descended the steps, not stopping until he reached the back door. Pushing through it, he breathed deeply, letting a rush of brisk, damp air penetrate to the deepest cells of his lungs.

"Is something the matter, sir?"

He turned at the sound of Richard's voice behind him. "No. Should there be?"

"No, sir."

David read the doubt in his butler's eyes. It was uncanny the way the man read his moods—uncanny and at times extremely disconcerting. Not that David had ever considered himself a complex person. He simply did what he had to do in order to survive, a skill he'd been forced to learn at a very young age.

Reaching into his pocket, Richard retrieved a white handkerchief and dusted the seats of a couple of wrought-iron garden chairs. "Why don't you have a seat, sir? Let me fix you a martini."

"Not yet. I just want to watch the sun set."

Richard settled in one of the chairs and undid the top button of his shirt. After five, he tended to be slightly more relaxed, though David had never requested or understood his need to be more formal during the day. It wasn't as if they ever had unexpected guests drop by for tea.

"I thought the day went well," Richard said. "I like Becca Smith. What do you think of her?"

The question caught him off guard. Not because he hadn't considered it, but because he had considered it so frequently since the first night he'd spotted her leaving her shop, head high, unafraid even when she'd noticed him in the shadows. She'd looked him in the eye and met his gaze.

The moment lasted briefly, yet something strange and incomprehensible had passed between them. He'd felt it in every part of his body, and the unfamiliar feelings had left him so shaken, he'd missed his turn on the way home. Driving as if in a trance, he'd wound up five miles past the winding road to the Bluffs.

Now, weeks later, he still couldn't get her out of his mind. In five years, no woman had elicited any interest for him. But with one look, Becca had cast a spell on him that he seemed powerless to break.

"She's open and direct and she has lots of ideas for the Bluffs," Richard said. "I think she'll do an excellent job."

"I don't see any reason why she wouldn't." David stared at the horizon, at the sprays of orange-and-gold bands that painted the undersides of the puffy clouds. "I hope the two of you will be able to work together agreeably on this project."

"I think she'd prefer working with you."

"I doubt that very seriously," David said, finally turning back to face his butler. "Besides, I don't deal well with people anymore."

"You deal well with me." Richard crossed one leg over the other and leaned back in his chair. "I think you'd do fine with her. You'll never know unless you give yourself a chance."

David touched his fingers to the side of his face, bitterly aware of the effect it had had on the nurses in the hospital when they'd been forced to change the dressings on his wounds and deal with the countless skin grafts.

And his face, as disfigured as it was, was no match for the blotchy red patches of skin that covered his stomach like some infectious disease. "My chances ran out five years ago, Richard. I've learned to live with the fact."

"Have you?"

"Yes." At least his mind had accepted the truth. Until Becca came along, his heart and body had, as well. Surely, in time, it would be that way again.

The wind picked up, tearing dry leaves from the branches of the trees and sending them flying in an avalanche of golds, reds and browns. "Fall has definitely arrived," David said, past ready to change the subject.

"Yes. Time for McFarland Leary to rise from the grave."

"The guy has been buried since the late 1600s. He's probably already come back—as a handful of dust."

Richard rubbed his right hand along his jaw. "Not if the locals are right. They say he was consort to a witch. When she caught him cheating on her with a mortal woman, she damned him to an eternity of torment. Not only that, but he still seeks revenge on Moriah's Landing for claiming he was a warlock and sentencing him to death."

"I know. I've heard it all since I was a child. He supposedly comes back every five years and kills a young woman or two, to exact revenge on the town and in hopes the sacrifice will appease the witch so that she'll set him free. Mostly it's a tale for the tourists, but I'm sure there are some poor superstitious folk in the town who actually believe that nonsense, even though the facts don't bear it out. There have been no unsolved murders in town in twenty years."

"There's already talk in town that it was Leary who

killed the woman whose body was found on Old Mountain Road last night.''

''How did you hear that?''

''I stopped at the grocers when I took Becca back to Threads.''

''And while they're worried about a ghost, some dangerous lunatic is running around free.''

''So is the man who abducted and tortured Claire Cavendish five years ago.''

''Surely you haven't succumbed to ghost tales.''

''No. I don't believe Leary's responsible for any of those horrors, but there's something evil and angry in Moriah's Landing. I can never put my finger on it, but it's always present, as if the heart of the town is beating inside a madman.''

David had no argument for that. The evil was in the black heart of a killer who'd destroyed his world. The anger and the madness lived inside him. He took one last look as the rays from the setting sun glanced off the rocks along the cliff. ''I think I'll go for a walk,'' he said, standing and stretching his weak leg.

''Would you like dinner at seven?''

''Let's make it eight tonight.''

''Whatever you say.''

Would that all of his life were that easy. If it were, he'd be with Becca Smith tonight. His body came alive at the thought, the need inside him so strong it rocked through him with the force of a tidal wave, making it difficult for him to keep walking.

He shouldn't want her this way. He had no right. Even if he wasn't still in love with Tasha, he had nothing at all to give Becca Smith. He was forty. She was surely no more than in her early twenties. He was scarred and hideous. She was young and beautiful, with her whole life in front of her. He was the Beast. She was Beauty.

And he'd given up believing there would ever be a happy ending for him five years ago.

But he wouldn't give up on having her near him. He couldn't. Not yet.

Chapter Four

Becca arrived at the Beachway Diner at ten before seven. The place was less crowded than it would have been during the week. Dates went to the more classy Crow's Nest for Saturday dinner and families took advantage of the gorgeous fall weather to drive up in the mountains for the weekend or to barbecue hot dogs and steaks on their back decks.

But the diner would pick up later, when craggy old fishermen needed some food to soak up the whiskey they'd been tossing down their throats and when the college kids and locals tired of the carnival and came wandering in for hot bowls of chowder and steaming mugs of apple cider.

Becca scanned the area and spotted Brie Pierce and Elizabeth Ryan at a table in the back. The sight reassured her and took away some of the chill she'd experienced while reading the sparse details of the murders from twenty years ago. She'd met lots of people since moving to Moriah's Landing just under a year ago, but Brie, Elizabeth, Kat and Claire were the only ones she'd call true friends.

Brie looked up and waved her over. Becca waved back and started in their direction. Her pumps clicked along the slick coating of grease that had accumulated on the plank flooring over the years, and she wished she had on her loafers the way she usually did when she came here. Comfortable jeans and a sweater would have been nice, too. As it was, she was seriously overdressed.

"Are you meeting someone?" Brie asked, as soon as she could be heard above the splattering of meat patties on the grill and the clattering coming from the kitchen.

"Claire Cavendish."

"Then join us," Elizabeth insisted. "Drew's speaking to a group of students at Heathrow and Cullen's on duty tonight."

"And they trust you two out on the town?" Becca teased, sliding into one of the two empty chairs at their table.

A blast of cold air circulated as the front door swung open. Becca turned, but the newest customers were a couple of uniformed cops. She directed her attention back to her friends, hoping she hadn't made a mistake about the time or the place she'd arranged to meet Claire.

The conversation stayed light, tiptoed along the edges of the murder, though Becca was certain it was in the backs of both Elizabeth's and Brie's minds. Elizabeth was a few years younger than Brie, though they had both been freshmen at Heathrow at the same time as Tasha, Kat and Claire. Becca had heard that Elizabeth's IQ fell somewhere in the genius range and she'd earned her Ph.D. in criminology by the age most students got their undergraduate degrees. With her long brown hair and flawless complexion, she looked more like a student than the professor she was.

Every time the door opened, Becca turned, but after ten minutes, there was still no sign of Claire. If she'd forgotten or changed her mind, that was fine, but Becca couldn't help but worry that something might be wrong.

Brie pushed a clump of curly red hair back from her face. "What time were you meeting Claire?" she asked, her green eyes shadowed and her usual quick smile drawn into a worried frown.

Becca was certain they were picking up on her apprehension. "Seven."

"Then I'm certain she'll be here any minute. It's only ten after, and promptness was never one of Claire's virtues." Brie squeezed a wedge of lemon into her iced tea and stirred the mixture, sending the ice cubes chasing around the inside of the glass. "Drew and I were just commenting earlier today on how well Claire's doing. I think the fact that you've befriended her has helped a lot."

"I hope," Becca said. "It's hard to tell. Some days she seems fine, but others she gets lost so deeply in one of her depressed moods, I can't seem to reach her at all."

Elizabeth nodded. "It's the same for me. I keep thinking it's because I was one of the girls there the night she was abducted, that by just being with her, I bring on the depressed moods."

"I doubt that's it," Brie said. "I know she needs her friends now, the new and the old. I'm certain she's upset by the news of the body that was found on Old Mountain Road."

"We all are," Elizabeth said.

"I know, but I don't want to think about the murder tonight," Brie said. "It's just too terrible, as if the horror of five years ago is about to start all over again."

"No one was murdered five years ago," Elizabeth reminded her.

"I know, but Claire was abducted and she'll never be the same again. And then poor Tasha was killed in that horrible explosion. And look at David Bryson. He's been wounded, slinking around in the shadows and never having anything to do with anyone in town.

"David's not so different." Becca felt the glare of her friends even before she'd gotten the whole sentence out of her mouth. She'd been too assertive, sounded more like a defense lawyer than a casual observer. "I mean, he's probably just more comfortable staying out of crowds."

"He does more than stay out of crowds," Elizabeth reminded her. "He stays out of town altogether during the daylight, and when he does come to town, he hangs out by himself in the shadows." Elizabeth stared at the front of the diner, then turned and put a hand on Brie's arm. "Isn't that Drew's uncle standing at the cash register?"

Brie turned. "That's Geoffrey Pierce, all right. I'm surprised to see him in here. He never came in when I was working here."

"Aren't you going to go over and say hello?" Becca asked.

"I don't think so. We haven't been on the best of terms since I heard him accuse Drew of marrying me just to avert a scandal. Not that he has that much to do with any of the Pierce family anymore. Mostly, he stays at the beach house."

Becca watched Geoffrey. He was in his mid-forties with thinning blond hair and a wiry mustache and beard that made him look ten years older than the last time she'd see him. In fact, if Elizabeth hadn't said something, she doubted she'd have recognized him at all. His eyes were narrowed as he paid the cashier, and he had an air about him that gave the impression he was not to be messed with. Still, he'd been polite and very attentive the few times Becca had met him.

"Was there a falling out between him and the rest of the family?" Elizabeth asked as Geoffrey finished paying his tab and left the diner.

"Not exactly, but Drew doesn't fully trust him. He thinks he may have been involved in some of Dr. Leland Manning's projects, though Geoffrey's denied it."

Becca listened to the talk. She found the Pierces fascinating. If it was true that every town had one family that seemed to be the rulers, the Pierces were definitely that family in Moriah's Landing. Not only were they the founding family, they were the wealthiest and most influential in town. A close-knit group, they all lived in the same area of town, a huge walled-in family compound with a number of private homes clustered around a parklike setting that had served as the backdrop for Drew and Brie's garden wedding.

The largest home in the compound belonged to William and Maureen. William was a United States senator, already a local legend. His son Drew was running for mayor and, according to the polls, was going to win by a landslide.

She hoped it worked out like that. Of all the Pierces that she'd met, Drew was her favorite, especially since he'd married Brie, his first love from the wrong side of the tracks. Theirs was a true Cinderella story. Brie had worked as a waitress in the Beachway Diner up until Drew had found out that Brie's young daughter was his. Now he and Brie were as happy as any couple Becca had ever seen.

The door opened again and this time it was Claire who stepped inside, and the minute she did, Becca was certain she had not had a good day. Her face seemed paler than usual, and her eyes were red as if she'd been crying.

But no matter what had spooked her, Becca was certain that wouldn't keep her from making Becca's meeting with David Bryson the main topic of conversation.

DINNER WITH CLAIRE turned out to be a very bad idea. As Brie had feared, news of the murder had really upset her. She was distracted, lost in her own thoughts for much of the meal, barely touching her food or even trying to make conversation with any of them.

And, just as Becca had feared, when Claire did talk, it was to beg her not to go back to the Bluffs. Brie and Elizabeth jumped right into that conversation, questions popping as quickly and as randomly as kernels of corn in a hot skillet. Neither of them felt as negatively about David but they agreed that Becca's working for him was asking for trouble.

For the first time since Becca had settled in Moriah's Landing, she was beginning to think she might have made a mistake in moving to such a small town. She wasn't used to having people tell her how to handle her business. But then, she wasn't used to anyone's caring about her safety, either. Perhaps it was a fair trade-off. Still, she was thankful when they paid the bill and exited the restaurant.

A gust of cold wind whipped Becca's hair into her face as she and Claire started the short walk home. The saltwater-laced mist burned her nostrils and pricked her flesh.

"It's cold for September," Claire said, pulling her jacket tighter. "The old fishermen always say that's an omen that the winter will be harsh."

Becca linked her right arm with Claire's left one. "I

like the feel of fall in the air," she said, hoping to dispel the spirit of gloom and doom that hovered over Claire. "It makes me think of pumpkin pies, steaming cups of hot chocolate and bonfires."

"I hate September. I dread to see it come and don't breathe easy until it's over."

"Then let's make a pact, Claire. You and me."

"What kind of pact?"

"A promise that we'll do something wonderfully fun every September."

"What will we do?"

"We could throw a party. Or go to Boston on a shopping excursion. Or we could pitch tents on the beach and have a slumber party. Roast wieners and marshmallows and make s'mores."

"No. No camping out. Not for me. The last time I spent the night outside was when...you know, that night..."

"Oh, gads. I'm sorry. My mouth flew into gear before my brain. Absolutely no camping. And you don't have to explain anything about that night to me."

"Thanks."

They walked the next block in silence. Becca concentrated on the sound of their feet against the pavement, the thud of Claire's loafers, the click of Becca's black pumps. A foghorn sounded in the distance and the strains of a poignant love song escaped through the open doors of Wheels.

Turning her head, she caught sight of the lights shining through the windows of the Bluffs. For a second she imagined herself sitting on one of the Victorian sofas in the rectangular drawing room that extended almost to the very edge of the cliff. The only light in the room came from the yellow flames that danced in the massive fireplace and the flickering glow of candles resting on the hand-carved mantel.

A shadow crossed the room and David stepped in front of her and put out his hand. "May I have this dance?"

Her heart jumped to her mouth, then plunged to the pit of her stomach. Reeling from the emotion, she shook her head, forcing the images to recede. She had no idea where they'd come from or why they seemed so real. She did know that they were not the kind of thoughts she should be having about a man she barely knew.

"He's a vampire, or at the very least a warlock."

She tugged Claire to a stop. "What are you talking about? Who's a warlock?"

"I'm talking about David Bryson, of course. You were thinking about him, weren't you?"

"Maybe."

"Not maybe. You were."

"Okay. I was thinking of him, but how did you know that?"

"I saw you staring at the Bluffs."

Becca breathed a sigh of relief, glad she hadn't admitted how Claire's seemingly clairvoyant statement had shaken her. She started walking again.

"Oh, Becca, I hate even thinking of your being up there in that horrible house. And no matter what you say about David Bryson, he's creepy and dangerous. I've heard he's cloning some kind of two-headed creature in that secret lab of his."

"Whatever he's doing in the lab, I won't have to worry about it. His butler made it clear that I'm to work only on the rooms he showed me today. They're all in the east wing, far away from the lab."

"Nothing you can say will make me feel good about your working for David Bryson."

"Your friend Tasha was in love with him. He can't be all bad."

"Tasha was bewitched by him, and the same thing is happening to you. I knew it the second I saw you staring at his house. You had the same look on your face that I saw on hers when she first met him."

"I'm not bewitched." Only she had experienced some strange surge of emotion when the images of her and David had taken shape in her mind. And she had this crazy desire to see him again when everyone she knew advised against it. "It's just a job," she reiterated, as much for her own benefit as for Claire's. "I probably won't even run into Dr. Bryson again. According to his butler, the man spends most of the daylight hours in his lab."

"In his *dark,* lab, I bet. How creepy can you get?"

Becca shook her head. She couldn't explain why she was going back to the Bluffs, not rationally. The money, the job. They were the excuses, but not the reasons.

A black cat ran out from the bushes and darted in front of them. Claire grabbed her arm and tugged her to a stop. "The cat is an omen, Becca. He's trying to tell us something."

Becca shook her head, suddenly weary with dealing with Claire's superstitions and fears. "It's only a cat."

"A black cat."

"A very pretty black cat." She started walking again.

Claire followed reluctantly. "We shouldn't take the path the cat just crossed."

"We should if we want to get home."

Claire seemed to settle down, or at least she kept walking and stopped talking about the horrors of September and bad omens. They were passing by the secluded area now, empty lots on both sides of the street with big trees and spreading branches that creaked in the wind.

But tonight there was a different sound, a crunching, like footfalls crushing dry leaves. Becca stopped and turned. There was no movement except the shadowy blur of moonlight filtering through the branches that quivered in the wind.

"Is something wrong?" Claire asked

"I thought I heard footsteps behind us."

Claire tensed instantly and gripped Becca's hand. "It's *him.*"

"It's no one, Claire." She said the words with as much authority as she could muster, considering the fact that she didn't believe them herself. "Just keep walking. We'll be home in a few minutes."

But Claire didn't keep walking. She stood, shaking, her eyes wide and wild. "You can't run from him. You scream and you scream, but he never stops. He just never stops."

Poor Claire. She was drifting back into the nightmare, moving and talking as if in a trance, and Becca could almost feel the horror as it wrapped Claire inside its tormenting shell. But if someone was back there, they needed to keep moving. "Everything's okay, Claire. Just keep walking."

Claire seemed to sink into herself, become a little girl, a very frightened little girl.

"One more block," Becca coaxed, trying to pull her along. "That's all. We'll be able to see your house as soon as we turn the corner. I bet your mother left the porch light on for you."

But someone was definitely behind them now, to the

left, hidden in the trees and darkness. She couldn't run off and leave Claire. The little she knew about self-defense raced through her mind, and she reached down and picked up a broken branch that was little more than a twig.

"Leave us alone," she ordered, waving her branch like a sword. There was movement, but still she couldn't make out the form of a man. "You're frightening my friend."

"It's you who should be afraid this time."

"It's him," Claire whispered. "It's him." A second later she collapsed into a terrified ball at Becca's feet, leaving Becca to face the man alone.

Chapter Five

Becca held tight to the brittle limb, waving it over her head. She'd go for the eyes first and try to get a knee to the crotch. But even if she landed a perfect blow, it wouldn't help for long. She couldn't take off and leave Claire to the man's mercy.

"I'll throw my purse down. You can take what money I have, and I won't even report the theft," she said, hoping against hope that her offer might appease him.

"I don't want your money." The man stepped toward them, though still not into the open. She could see the outline of his frame, lean, not particularly tall—threatening. She struggled to catch her breath and to get a glimpse of his face, but his features blended into the shadowy backdrop as if he were faceless.

Leary rises from the dead every five years and comes for his victims. The terrifying legend seared itself into her brain as terror swelled inside her. She stood, deathly still, unable to move. But even in the midst of the terror, she knew this wasn't a ghost, and he wouldn't vanish in a puff of smoke.

"What do you want from us?" she asked.

"Satisfaction."

Becca tried to tug Claire to a standing position, but

Claire continued to sit in the middle of the sidewalk, rocking back and forth, her knees cradled in her arms.

"You should be worried about yourself instead of that sniveling—"

The spray of headlight beams and the sound of a car engine interrupted his words. She turned to see a sleek sports car slowing to a crawl. Adrenaline rushed through Becca, finally breaking the stifling hold of fear. She left Claire and dashed into the street, waving her hands and screaming for help. She could hear the footsteps of their would-be attacker, running in the opposite direction as the car came to a screeching halt. The door of the low-slung sports car swung open, and Geoffrey Pierce jumped out.

"Becca, is that you?"

"Yes. And Claire Cavendish." Her voice skidded along the edges of her choppy breath. "Someone tried to attack us."

He scanned the area without stepping away from his car. "Where is he?"

"In that vacant lot." She pointed to the area she'd last seen the man. "But he's gone. He ran off when we saw the lights of your car."

"Damn. I knew something like this would happen."

"What are you talking about?"

"You, traveling up to the Bluffs."

"How do you know about that?"

"There are no secrets in Moriah's Landing. Remember that, along with the fact that you can't mess around with the likes of David Bryson and just walk away unscathed. The man's evil through and through."

"It wasn't David Bryson."

"Then who was it?"

"I don't know, but it wasn't David."

"Did you get a good look at the man? Could you identify him if you saw him again?"

"No. All I really saw was shadows." Becca looked back at Claire. She still sat huddled on the cold concrete, hugging her knees, her head buried in the folds of her arms. Becca walked over and wrapped an arm around Claire's shoulder. "It's all right, Claire. Geoffrey Pierce is here to help us now. No one will hurt you."

Claire looked up at Geoffrey, her eyes wide. A low scream gurgled from her lips, then faded in a series of hard shudders.

"We need to get her home," Geoffrey said. "Let me help you."

Taking control, Geoffrey walked over and placed his hand out to Claire. She jerked away from him, whimpering like a frightened puppy. Somehow, Becca managed to get her to her feet. "Geoffrey Pierce is going to give us a ride home," she whispered. "The bad man is gone."

"No. Not again," Claire pleaded, her voice low and so shaky Becca could barely make out the words. "Don't leave me. Please, don't leave me."

Becca held her tight. "It's okay, sweetie. I won't leave you. Just lean on me, and I'll help you into the car."

Claire moved as if in a trance, trembling so that it was all Becca could do to get her to take the few steps to the car. Geoffrey tried to help, but Claire jerked away every time he tried to touch her. Becca crawled into the small back seat beside Claire and cradled her in her arms, stroking the back of her head with a steady hand.

"Whoever abducted her before sure did a number on her," Geoffrey said, once they were buckled into their seats. "Someone should hang that man by his toes and let the buzzards feast on him." He started the car and drove slowly down the street. "If you didn't get a good look at your attacker, Becca, how can you be so certain it wasn't David Bryson?"

"I would have known David's voice." That was factual, but it only scratched the surface of the full truth. If David had been standing there, she would have felt his aura, that strange awareness that churned inside her when he was near or even when she thought of him.

He turned onto Front Street. Sure enough, the porch light was on. Mrs. Cavendish always left the light on until the last of her children were safely in for the night. She did the same for Becca since she'd moved in with them.

"That's Claire's house, the one with the porch light on," Becca said.

"I know. I used to drive Tasha over here to see Claire back before Tasha was old enough to drive. The two of them were good friends since grade school. I remember how upset Tasha was when Claire was abducted. A few weeks later, Tasha was dead. All because she got mixed up with David Bryson."

The bitterness crept into his voice. Becca was sure he missed Tasha. The whole Pierce family had evidently loved her very much. The whole town had, but she doubted if any of them loved her any more than David had.

Geoffrey pulled to a stop in front of the house, killed the motor and turned to Becca. "I'm begging you to stay away from the Bluffs and from David Bryson, Becca."

"I'm sure David means me no harm."

"Then you are far too trusting. You're a beautiful woman, soft and kind. Trusting, the way Tasha was.

That's just the kind of woman he likes, someone he can sweep off her feet with his money and pseudo sophistication. But bear in mind that he is a fake, a dangerous, *deadly* fake.''

His words seemed to catch and stick in the night air, lingering after his voice had become silent. Becca knew he expected a promise that she'd heed his warning, but she couldn't do that—not yet—so she said nothing. He turned, opened the driver-side door and crawled from behind the wheel as Becca pushed the door open on Claire's side. Geoffrey put a hand out to help Claire. She trembled and pulled away from him.

"It's probably better if I can get her up the steps by myself," Becca said. "She'll feel safer with me."

"I can understand that."

He stepped out of the way as Becca struggled to get Claire out of the cramped back seat and onto the sidewalk. She had stopped whimpering, but she still clung to Becca and didn't seem able to bear the full weight of her body.

Becca turned back to Geoffrey as they reached the door. He was waiting at the foot of the steps, watching, ready to help if she needed him. "Thanks, again. I don't know how I'll ever repay you for this."

"Stay away from Bryson."

"I'll think about it."

"Which means you won't. You're already under his spell. May God keep you safe. He's the only one who can." He turned and got back into his car.

"May God keep us all safe," she whispered as she knocked on the door. She had a key, but couldn't get to it and hold Claire erect, too.

A few seconds later, Mrs. Cavendish opened the door. One look at Claire and the woman's eyes welled with tears. She took Claire in her arms and rocked her against her ample chest.

"My baby. My poor baby. What's happened now?"

Becca took a deep breath. There was no easy way to explain what had happened to Claire, certainly no way to make Mrs. Cavendish feel a bit better.

Claire had called it right about September. Fall in Moriah's Landing was like a cruise through a carnival chamber of horrors. And there was no getting off the ride.

IT WAS TWO HOURS LATER before Becca was able to go to her room and have a minute to herself. Now, showered and dressed for bed, she stared out the window and let her mind meander through the events of the evening.

Once they'd been free of the actual danger, the hardest part had been watching Claire draw back into her shell, become almost comatose as her mother tried desperately to reassure her that everything was okay. And as difficult as it was to watch Claire, it was equally hard to watch the pain and heartbreak settle into every line of Mrs. Cavendish's face.

Becca had left Claire to her mother's care while she called the police to report the incident. The first policeman had arrived in minutes. He was young, polite and amazingly efficient. His questions had been direct and to the point and he'd taken Becca's every response at face value.

Ten minutes after he'd finished with his questions and left the house, Detective Carson Megham had shown up. The man was at least sixty, had droopy eyes, a fat neck, chewed incessantly on an unlit cigar, and all his questions seemed to come from left field. He'd stayed thirty minutes, drunk the coffee Mrs. Cavendish offered and filled one page of his notebook with lines and squiggles and very few notes.

When he left, Becca was certain that in all her life, she'd never been so glad to see the door close behind any man. She took a deep breath and tried to find something more pleasant to fill her mind before she climbed into bed.

Claire was sleeping now. The rest of the household seemed to be, as well. And if Becca didn't get some sound sleep soon herself, she'd be a wasted wreck tomorrow when she needed to be fully alert and laying out a plan for redecorating the Bluffs.

She stretched and walked over to the bed. Either she was wrong about David, or Geoffrey Pierce and everyone else in town were mistaken. Maybe she was bewitched.

Thoughts of David pushed away the fright of the night like nothing else had. She climbed into bed, snuggled under the covers and pictured him scattering white roses on top of the cliff. Images coalesced and floated through her mind. She imagined the way David had looked five years ago when Tasha had fallen completely under his spell. He'd been so handsome, her young heart had probably melted at his first touch, the thrill of his first kiss.

Emotions toppled over one another, dizzying, titillating. Tasha had probably never had a chance to do anything but fall in love with David. If Becca wasn't very careful, she might fall in love with him, too. She was already infatuated with the man.

A man who lived in the shadows, shrouded in mystery. Captivating. Mesmerizing. Dark.

THE MUSIC WAS HAUNTING, a love song that dipped inside Becca and stirred her soul. The room was lit only by the glow of candles on the marble hearth and a fire that licked the logs and danced recklessly inside the massive fireplace.

David held out his hand and Becca slipped into his arms. She felt the pressure of his hand on the small of her back, pulling her closer. Her heart beat against his chest. Her belly rubbed against his, and their thighs did their own dance, a touch and retreat that awakened every erogenous zone in her body.

He tucked a thumb under her chin and tilted her face toward his. Desire blazed in his eyes, then swelled inside her until she felt the moisture pool and begin to flow inside her. He put his mouth to hers, and when he spoke she felt the quick flick of his tongue on the flesh of her earlobe. *"I wish this night could last forever,"* he whispered. *"Just the two of us suspended in time."*

"It can last. We'll make it last."

"Promise that. Promise me you'll always love me the way you love me tonight."

"Make love with me, David."

"I can't. Not yet."

"Please. I can't bear it if you don't."

His lips touched hers, and the thrill of the kiss swept through her in a silken rush. She wanted him so, imagined him ripping her clothes from her body and taking her right there in front of the fire that blazed in the massive fireplace. Instead he pulled away. *"You'll have to go now, Becca."*

"No. Please. I need you, David."

"If you stay, I'll hurt you."

"No. You'll never hurt me. You couldn't."

"But I will."

"Becca."

His voice had changed and his face had erupted into

a glaring mass of red, mottled skin and jagged scars. He was hideously frightening, totally macabre. She started to run, but she couldn't get away. His footsteps were pounding behind her.

Pounding louder and louder.

"Becca, are you awake?"

She opened her eyes and pushed wet strands of hair from her face, confusion twisting inside her like rusty coils.

The pounding started again. "Becca, you have a phone call."

Tommy Cavendish? Claire's brother. Shaking from the emotions stirred by the dream, she rolled over and looked around, half expecting to see David lying beside her. Needless to say, he wasn't there.

"Who's calling at this hour?" she called, her voice heavy from sleep and the aftermath of passion and fear.

"It's not all that early, lazybones. It's after eight. And it's some guy, but he didn't give his name. Want me to take a message?"

"No. I'll take the call." She slid her feet to the floor and into her slippers. Grabbing her old flannel robe from the hook on the door, she slung it over her shoulders and shoved her arms through the sleeves.

A man? She couldn't imagine who would be calling her on Sunday morning. It couldn't be Larry. Tommy would have recognized his voice. She just hoped it wasn't Detective Megham. Anyone but him.

"Better grab the family room extension, that is if you want to hear," Tommy said, when she started toward the kitchen. "Mom's cooking pancakes and the little ones are helping."

"Gotcha."

She breathed in the invigorating odors of fresh-brewed coffee and bacon and hurried to the family room.

"Hello."

"Good morning, Becca. I hope I didn't wake you."

David's voice dipped inside, revived the dream, and she went weak. "No," she answered, hoping the huskiness of sleep camouflaged her feelings. "Is something wrong?"

"I heard what happened last night to you and Claire."

"News travels fast in Moriah's Landing."

"Especially bad news. Are you all right?"

"I'm fine. I'm not so sure about Claire, though. I haven't had a chance to check on her this morning, but she went all to pieces last night, collapsed into a quivering mass of terror."

"I'm sorry to hear that."

"Is that why you called? To ask about last night?"

"No. I need to see you."

"I'm planning to come back out to the Bluffs tomorrow to get some more measurements."

"I'd like to see you this morning."

"When?"

"When can you be ready?"

"I just woke up. I'm not dressed, and I haven't had breakfast."

"You can have breakfast with me. I'll send Richard to pick you up."

The recluse who never left the shadows wanted her company for breakfast. But why, especially when he had barely bothered to visit with her when she'd been at the Bluffs? It was all too bizarre.

"Please, Becca. It's important that I see you."

The persistent tone mingled with the hypnotic quality

of his voice, pulling her in as surely as if he'd reached out and caught her in his arms.

"I suppose I could—"

"Good," he interrupted. "Richard will be there in forty-five minutes."

Before she could answer, he'd broken the connection. Geoffrey Pierce's warning skirted along her nerve endings as she rushed to take a shower. But long before she'd slipped out of her robe and pajamas and climbed under the pulsating spray, the apprehension had been swallowed up by anticipation. She couldn't wait to see him again.

THE DAY WAS OVERCAST and gray, but even the little sunlight that managed to penetrate the heavy layers of clouds was blocked from the massive sitting room by the thick, opaque draperies that had been pulled tight and clamped to keep even a ribbon of sunlight from pushing its way through. The only illumination in the room was the flickering glow from a couple of candles that rested on top of the black marble mantel.

Dark, gloomy, the only place where David would feel comfortable entertaining Becca Smith. He hadn't planned on calling her this morning at all, but he'd lain awake for hours last night, hating that some monster had come so close to her that he had left her running to the likes of Geoffrey Pierce for help. He could have lost her, could have been awakening to the news that her body had been discovered in the woods, two slashes cut through her jugular, left to be found by animals or boys on dirt bikes.

The travesty would have been too great. To lose her forever when he ached to have her here where he could watch over her. He ached to touch her, to run his hands down the smooth lines of her face, to fit his lips against the back of her neck and feel her tremble in desire.

Desire for a monster, one almost twice her age? It would never happen, and still he couldn't let her go. His body stiffened as he heard footsteps in the hall and the sound of Becca's voice. It tinkled, the way Tasha's had, a bubbly, rich ringing sound that screamed youth and whispered naiveté.

So much like Tasha and yet so different. More self-assured, her curves more mature, her lips fuller. Her hair was the color of summer straw, where Tasha's had been like sunlight sparkling through morning mist.

A few seconds later, the door opened, and Becca stepped inside. He drew in a deep breath, steadying his voice, seeking a calm that wouldn't give away the intensity of his need. "Hello, Becca. Welcome back to The Bluffs."

BECCA HESITATED, giving her pupils time to adjust to increasing darkness. A chill of apprehension darted up her backbone, froze her to the spot, as she let her gaze move around the cavernous room. Richard's footsteps were receding. She was alone with David.

He sat on the floor on a satin blanket stretched in front of the unlit fireplace, his face shadowed, his eyes capturing darting reflections from the candles' glow. "It's so dark I can barely see you," she whispered, realizing that fear had left her almost too breathless to speak. "Do you mind if I turn on the light?"

"I prefer the darkness, and there are no lights in this room."

"Then it's true what people say about you."

"I never bother myself with what people say. But what is it that concerns you?"

"They say you only go out at night."

"They're mistaken. I went for a horseback ride at daybreak."

So the tales weren't true, or else he was lying. He was definitely in the dark now, and she was in here with him. Alone in an isolated area of a seventy-room fortress at the tip of a cliff. But no one had forced her to come. She'd come willingly, and even now, she eased closer instead of running away.

"I hope you're hungry," he said, motioning to the feast spread out beside him.

"I'm not sure I can eat at all."

"If you don't like the food we can have Richard bring something else."

"Oh, no, it's not that. It's just that, I'm not sure about you, David. I mean, I'm not sure I can trust you."

"Are you afraid I'll seduce you?"

Yes. Afraid he would. Afraid he wouldn't. "I'm not sure what I'm afraid of. You're different from any man I've ever known."

"Have you known so many?"

"Of course not. I mean I've known them, but I haven't been *with* a lot of men."

"I'm glad. And you don't have to be afraid of me. I'd never hurt you, at least not intentionally."

"Then I guess we should have breakfast and talk." She stared at the food, amazed at the variety of selections and the amount. "Are you sure you didn't tell Richard you were feeding a few dozen guests?" she said, striving to regain some control over her emotions and lighten the mood.

"I told him it was for two, but he tends to go overboard with this sort of thing."

"Do you do this often?"

"Eat breakfast?"

"Invite a friend for an indoor picnic."

"Once every decade or so. Actually you're probably the only person in town who would have accepted the invitation."

"Does it bother you that the people in Moriah's Landing seem to fear you?"

"Not anymore, and they don't all fear me. The Pierces merely hate me—and make sure I'm kept in my place."

So, he knew how Tasha's family felt about him. It must make her death all the harder on him. "Have you tried to mend fences with them?"

"Not really. We weren't friends when Tasha was alive. I see no reason for us to become friends now."

"They're a huge family. I don't think you should lump them altogether like a barrel of spoiled fish."

"I don't. I actually like Drew Pierce and think he'll make a good mayor. And though I have no use for Geoffrey Pierce, I'm glad he showed up for you and Claire last night."

"Still, it must bother you that Tasha's family seems to hold you responsible for her death."

"I don't worry much about any of the Pierces. I have my work, and my memories. That's more than a lot of people have. Besides, this lifestyle suits me."

She couldn't imagine that a lifestyle devoid of friends and relationships suited anyone, but she didn't want to pry into what made him tick. Not yet. It was enough that they would be working together and that she was getting to know him little by little.

David pushed a plate in her direction. "Help yourself to the food. And there's coffee or champagne."

"Champagne sounds wonderful."

"Then champagne it is."

He lifted the bottle from an insulated carrying case, then pointed it away from them and popped the cork. His hands were smooth, his fingers long and steady, and she marveled that they'd missed the destructive effects of the explosion.

With that thought, her gaze went to his face. Even in the darkness, she could make out the curdled flesh along the right side of his face and a jagged-edged scar that seemed to suck his flesh into a hard line of resistance. Still brutally damaged after five years. It made her cringe even to imagine what his face must have looked like immediately after the explosion.

The effects would fade in time, or for all she knew, he might have more surgeries planned to correct the disfigurement. But there were likely other scars. Some on his body, some buried deep inside him. Becca knew more than she cared to about the kind of suffering and loss that buried itself deep inside a person's soul. She lived with it every day.

Still, she'd never even considered locking herself away from life the way David had done. But then she wasn't tormented by the memory of a lost love. Now that she thought about it, she was certain part of her infatuation with David had always been the idea of a man pining away for his one true love. The whole tortured-hero idea was straight out of the classics.

David looked up and she averted her gaze, hopefully before he realized that she'd been staring at him. He poured the champagne into two crystal flutes.

"How elegant," she said, taking one as he held it toward her. "If I'd known we were going formal, I would have dressed for the occasion."

"You look lovely just as you are. It's Richard who

has a flair for the elegant. I myself am a lifelong member of the Moriah's Landing Riffraff Club.''

''Riffraff don't live in castles.''

''They do in my case. In Moriah's Landing, a man never escapes the branding of his birth, and I'm not only from the wrong side of town—the wharf—but the back side of that. Not that some of the more prominent men in town didn't come slumming into my neighborhood on occasion—even some of the pious Pierces.''

''My background's not so wonderful, either.''

''I know.''

His response surprised her. She'd never shared her past, or lack of one, with anyone in Moriah's Landing. ''How would you know?''

He tensed and glanced away. ''I looked into your credentials for the redecorating job.''

''But you found out about my private life?''

''I know about your near brush with death.''

''You had me investigated?'' She turned away from him and stared at the wall of shadows, suddenly so irritated she could barely sit there and maintain any semblance of control.

''I'm certainly not judging you, Becca. How could I?''

''Okay, David, just so we're on the same page here, why don't you tell me exactly what you found out about my past?''

Chapter Six

David understood Becca's irritation but doubted the facts would ease any of her anger or alleviate her fears. The simple truth was he had wanted to know everything about her—where she'd come from, if she'd been married before, whom she'd loved. He'd hoped that knowing might somehow lessen his inexplicable attraction for her. Instead it had only made her more fascinating.

He stared at her, looking deep into her sapphire eyes. "I only found out the basics about you, Becca."

"That's all there is about me, David. Basics. Cold, terrifying facts."

"You were strangled, had your face smashed in, then buried alive. It must have been a horrible experience."

"So horrible that I evidently blocked it from my mind along with everything else in my life."

"So you have no memory at all of clawing your way out of the grave."

"No, my first memory is waking up in the hospital, but according to the farmer who found me on his land in Vermont, I was coated in dirt and dried blood, disoriented, wandering aimlessly just a few yards from the shallow grave where someone had left me, probably believing they'd killed me even before they covered me with earth.''

His heart tightened into a wrenching knot at the thought of Becca fighting for breath, struggling to hold on to life. ''It's a miracle you survived.''

''That's what the doctor said. The police tried to find out who I was and what had happened to me, but I was just one of those unsolved mysteries.''

''And you never remembered anything about what happened?''

''No, and I was afraid to dig into the past. For all I knew the man who'd tried to kill me would come back and finish the job if he realized I was still alive. So I made up a name for myself and when I was finally released from the hospital, one of the nurses who'd befriended me got me a job working with her mother in a family owned tailor's shop. That's how I learned to sew.'' She took a deep breath and sipped the champagne. ''Great credentials. So why did you hire me, David?''

He blurted out the truth. ''I don't care who you were or what you did in the past. I'm interested in the person you are now.''

''I haven't told anyone in Moriah's Landing about my past.''

''Nor have I.'' He reached out and took her hand. To his surprise, she didn't pull away. ''It must have been tough, waking up and not knowing who you were.''

''It was tougher knowing no one cared. There were no missing persons reports filed on me, no one calling all the hospitals to see if I'd been admitted when I didn't come home that night. No one to care if I lived or died.''

The irritation she'd experienced a few minutes ago dissolved into a sadness that was mirrored in the misty blue of her eyes. A knot formed in his throat. He shouldn't be letting himself get this close to Becca, but he couldn't pull away. Not yet. "A lot of people care about you now."

"Are you one of those people, David?"

"I care." It didn't change anything, didn't lessen his love for Tasha, didn't make him any less of a hideous monster, but he did care. "Whoever you were before, you're Becca Smith now. A beautiful, vivacious, loving person."

But she hadn't been beautiful immediately after her ordeal. He'd read the entire terrifying report. The police opinion was the man had attacked her and strangled her. Then when he'd started to bury her, he either realized she was still alive or just wanted to make certain she was dead. He'd smashed in her face, probably with the shovel, doing massive damage to the bones and tissue.

Fortunately, she'd ended up in a hospital connected to the medical school, providing her with some of the best care and reconstructive surgery available in the country—all at no cost to her.

She sipped her champagne. "I wish you'd trusted me, David, without an investigation."

"It's not a matter of trust. It's just a routine business arrangement."

"Like having me here for brunch in a room with the drapes pulled tight and the only light a faint glow from two flickering candles. There's nothing ordinary about you, David. Nothing ordinary about this."

He touched his hand to the sickening flesh and scar on the right side of his face. "A man does what he has to, Becca. Believe me, the sight of me in sunlight would not be pleasant."

"I'm not afraid to look at you."

"One day I may put you to the test, but not yet. Now, I suggest we eat before the food gets cold."

DAVID SQUEEZED HER HAND before letting go of it. Becca would have expected that his knowing about her past would have added a strain to their fragile relationship. Instead she felt a new bond with him. He was the one person in all the world who knew as much about her as she knew about herself.

Everything about their relationship was bizarre and mysterious, almost haunting, and yet there was no denying her attraction to him. She didn't know her own age, but she thought she must be in her early to midtwenties. David was forty. She was a working girl, lucky to have been given the opportunity to learn a trade that allowed her to support herself and provide the necessities of life. David was extremely wealthy.

Most of all, he was a recluse, a man who revealed so little of himself that it would be impossible for her to ever know the man behind the shadows and deformities. Yet here she was, with him by choice, having brunch in a setting straight from a horror movie.

He broke off a piece of crusty bread and slathered it with marmalade. But instead of placing it in his mouth, he reached across the space that separated them and held it to her lips. Becca opened her mouth and took a bite. When her lips accidentally brushed his fingers, her whole body reacted crazily, as racked by desire from that simple touch as it had been during last night's dream.

They both retreated into the task of eating, but David kept her champagne glass full. By the time she'd eaten all she could possibly hold, she was feeling warm and more than a little giddy. She had a ridiculous urge to reach across the blanket and link her fingers with his. She wondered what he'd do if she did.

But he was the one who made the first move. He reached out and trailed a finger down the sleeve of her sweater. "You look good in blue. It brings out your eyes."

She shook her head, pushed her long hair back from her face and managed a throaty thanks. If anyone else had given a casual compliment like that, she would hardly have noticed. Now she was feeling a glow that reached from her toes to the tip of her head.

He leaned over and touched her lips with his. Quick. Gentle. More like a hint than an actual kiss, yet she felt as if her insides had melted and turned inside out.

"Why did you do that?" she asked when her breath came back to her lungs.

"Because in spite of what the people in town say, I'm just a man."

Only he wasn't. She was sure of that now, at least he wasn't like any man she'd ever kissed before.

He picked up his near-empty glass and twirled the remaining liquid for mesmerizing moments before meeting her gaze again. When he did, his dark eyes seemed to whisper of secrets and regret. "I shouldn't have kissed you, Becca, but I do have a proposition for you."

"What kind of proposition?"

"If you're going to be working at the Bluffs, you should live here as well. It will save you travel time. Besides, why should you be cramped in a tiny room at the Cavendish home when we have so many rooms going unused?"

The idea was chilling, incredible. She'd walk out of her life and into David Bryson's—a world so linked to the past, it was as if he had become a ghost of a man lurking in candlelight and shadows.

"I can't possibly live here."

"You'd be safe from the kind of man you encountered last night."

"I'm not looking to run from life, David. I could never lock myself away behind stone walls, never give up my friends or the sunlight."

"I would never ask you to."

"It's out of the question. I'm willing to work for you, but that's it. I can't even consider living here."

"I'd hoped that you would. It would be better for all of us."

She stood and dusted bread crumbs from her jeans. "I don't know what you want from me, David, but whatever it is, I can't provide it. Perhaps I shouldn't take the job at all."

He stood. "Is that what you want, to just walk away and never return?"

She was trembling now, inside and out, part of her wanting to step into his arms and say she never wanted to leave, but the little bit of rationality she had remaining urged her to get out while she could. Leave before she was completely bewitched by David Bryson.

"I can't think about this now. Please, have Richard drive me home."

"Very well, Becca." He stood and walked toward the door. Before he opened it, he leaned against it, staring at her in the eerie grayness of the room. "If you ever change your mind, your room is waiting." With that, he opened the door and walked away.

She struggled to swallow past the lump in her throat. Her room was waiting. Bizarre images swam through her mind. A four-poster bed plump with feather mattresses, covered in an exquisite quilt. A crystal vase of white roses atop a polished mahogany dresser and silver picture frames of her and David. No. Not her. The snapshots were of David and Tasha.

Becca's lungs burned, and her legs grew wobbly. This place was haunted. There was no other explanation. Perhaps it was Tasha's ghost that filled the rooms and kept David chained to her even though she'd been dead for years.

The door opened again, but this time it was Richard. "Dr. Bryson says you're ready to go home."

"Home?"

"Back to the Cavendish residence."

She exhaled sharply. "Yes. I'm ready." Slowly her body and mind began to function in a halfway normal manner as she followed Richard down the long hall and toward the front door. The halls were empty, yet she sensed David's presence, felt he was watching her every step. And already she missed him.

Bewitched by a man with dark eyes and a voice that crawled inside her very soul? Just as Claire had predicted.

DAVID PACED THE LAB, unable to work, unable to think of anything except Becca. He didn't give a damn about having her work at the Bluffs. He merely wanted her there, wanted to watch her walk, listen to her talk, run his hands through the silky strands of her hair. Finish the kiss he'd barely started a few minutes earlier.

No. He shouldn't even think such inane thoughts. But Becca was like a drug that had gotten into his system and short-circuited his reasoning powers. He would have to meet a woman who affected him like this, now, of all times, when he was finally making progress in reaching the goal that drove his life.

He'd spent five years prowling lonely streets in the wee hours of the morning and hanging out in the shadows that obscured the wharf, searching for any clue as to the identity of the murderous rat who had caused the explosion that ruined his life and stole Tasha's. The police might call it an accident. He knew better.

But now he had the records Dr. Leland Manning had kept on the workings of the Moriah's Landing secret medical society, meticulous records outlining the many unethical research projects the society had conducted over the years and the way the members of the society had destroyed anyone and anything that got in their way.

Manning wouldn't be needing the records, not in the dirty cubicle of a prison cell where he would spend the rest of his life for illegal medical practices of his own. But, based on Manning's notes, David was almost certain that the society was connected to the explosion. The police had classified the explosion as an accident, but he'd checked the boat too thoroughly to buy that theory. He'd wanted to make certain nothing marred their honeymoon sailing trip.

Now it was only a matter of time until he unearthed the deadly secrets of hate and revenge and found the answers to his search. When he did, nothing in heaven or earth would stop him from getting his own sweet revenge, not even if it meant winding up in prison.

Just one more reason why he had to let Becca go. He had nothing to offer her. But still he felt the loss grinding away at what little was left of his soul. Becca had no past. He had way too much.

CARSON MEGHAM PULLED a half-crushed cigar from his pocket and poked it into his mouth. If Prissy saw him with it, she'd lay into him like the wildcat of a woman she was. Married thirty-five years and she still didn't give him a damn bit of room to cultivate his bad habits. But even Prissy might resort to a little comfort prop if she had to deal with the press in Moriah's Landing now that word had leaked out that the body found two days ago had been branded with the initials M.L.

He stood, stretched and walked to the door. If he'd been the chief, he'd find and fire the man who'd leaked the information. A bunch of hype about a murderous ghost was the last thing the investigation needed.

But it wasn't his decision to make. In spite of his years with the Kansas City police force, he was the new man on the totem pole in Moriah's Landing. Just a guy who'd finally given in to his wife's pleadings to retire and move back to the town where she'd grown up, only to find that life without a gun and a badge didn't cut it for him. This time he'd work until they forced him into retirement.

McFarland Leary? No way. This guy who'd cut the jugular on the Old Mountain Road body was flesh-and-blood and likely walking the streets right now looking for his next victim. Someone young and pretty. Someone like Becca Smith. She might have been seconds away from a body bag last night. The killer might even be someone she knew, someone who knew she'd be walking that route and passing the wooded lot.

Someone crazy. Out of control. Demented. Someone like Dr. David Bryson.

BECCA HAD RICHARD DROP her off at the corner nearest the Cavendish home, just in case Claire was on the porch or watching from a window. She'd been through enough last night and there was no reason to get her upset over Becca's being with David, especially since chances were good she wouldn't be seeing him again. The attraction she felt for him was dangerous and unrelenting. The only cure would be to put him out of her life completely.

That bit of news should make everyone in Moriah's Landing happy—Claire, Brie, Larry, Geoffrey, all the Pierces for that matter. So why couldn't she shake the terrible sense of loss, the ache that was already building inside her to see David again?

She groaned as she neared the house and realized that the dark green sedan sitting in front of the Cavendish home belonged to the same guy who'd come out to interview her last night. Not the nice uniformed officer who'd arrived first, but Detective Megham, the old goat who looked as if his face had been baked in a brick oven, though he was probably no more than sixty.

Hopefully he wasn't back here trying to interview Claire. Mrs. Cavendish had told him last night to leave Claire alone, that she wouldn't be able to tell him anything Becca hadn't. If that was why he was here, he'd find out quickly enough that he was no match for Mrs. Cavendish. A mother grizzly couldn't have been more ferocious at protecting her cubs than Mrs. Cavendish was at sheltering her emotionally wounded daughter.

Becca climbed the steps, preparing herself to go through last night's ordeal again when it was this morning's that seemed to have taken the biggest toll on her own emotional state. Just as she expected, the first thing she saw when she slipped through the front door was the detective sitting on the sofa, his arms spread over the back as if the seat were made for one instead of three.

Mrs. Cavendish was in the wooden rocker next to the

hearth, her usually cheerful face drawn into a distinct scowl. They both looked up and fastened their gazes on her when she stepped inside.

The detective stood and extended a hand. "Hello, Becca. Do you remember me? We met last night."

"Yes, I remember. Has something else happened?"

"No, I just needed to ask a few more questions, try to make sure I have everything straight in my mind."

"I told you everything I knew last night."

"I realize that, but sometimes people tend to forget a few details when they're so close to a situation. When the smoke settles, they sometimes remember little things that slipped their mind during the first questioning."

Mrs. Cavendish planted her feet firmly on the floor and stopped her chair from rocking. "He came here to talk to Claire. I've told him that's out of the question. She's practically catatonic today, just sitting in her room and staring out the window."

"It would help if I could talk to Claire, but I can wait," he answered. "But I want to talk to Becca again as well—alone, if you don't mind."

"If she says she's told you all she knows, then I'm sure she has. You shouldn't harangue the victims, Detective, especially a nice young lady like Becca."

Becca walked over and laid a hand on Mrs. Cavendish's shoulder, her fingers sliding into the loose weave of her oversize cardigan. The poor woman had enough to handle just taking care of her own brood without taking her on, as well. "It's fine, Mrs. Cavendish."

"Are you sure? Because I can sit right in here with you if you need me."

"No. I don't mind answering his questions, especially if he thinks it will help arrest the right man."

"Okay, dear, but if you need me, you just call."

She stood, and Becca could see that this latest trauma in Claire's life had left her mother's shoulders more stooped, as if the weight of watching her daughter's stability take its latest nosedive weighed almost more than she could bear. Becca took the rocker Mrs. Cavendish had previously occupied. "Fire when ready, Detective Megham."

He crossed his left foot over his right knee. "Why don't you just tell me exactly what you saw again? Try to place yourself back in the situation. I know it's not easy for you, but make it seem as real as possible."

She went through the story again, let the fear creep back inside her, relived the desperation when she realized that Claire couldn't even stand, much less run. And once again the grotesque image of a man who seemed to be born of the darkness—a man with no face—wormed its way into her mind. She didn't realize she was shaking until she finished the story.

Megham exhaled slowly, his mouth drawing into a disgusted sulk. "And that's all you remember? You can't describe the man at all."

"No. I never got a good look at him."

"That's too bad. If you could identify the man, it might all be over."

"You'd still have to catch him."

"If he's someone you know, that would probably be as easy as getting an arrest warrant and ringing a doorbell. If we could make an arrest, this town would sleep a lot easier tonight."

"If you arrest a man based on what I saw, you'd likely be arresting the wrong man."

"That's not what I'm aiming to do. I just want a killer off the street and behind bars before he strikes again."

"Then you think the man we saw last night might be

the man responsible for killing the woman whose body was found two nights ago?''

"I think there's a good chance. Isolated, unprovoked attacks on women are rare in this town."

"There have been other murders this year."

"All solved and none of them involving chance victims."

He was right, and it wasn't as if she hadn't had the same thought. Still, it bothered her to have her suspicions voiced by a detective. "Are you working the murder case as well?"

"Yeah." He uncrossed his leg, rested his elbows on his knees and leaned in close. "Just a couple of more questions, Becca. Do you know David Bryson?"

She felt a throb in her right temple, quick, pulsating, like a yellow caution light blinking a warning. "Why do you ask?"

"I take that as a yes."

She could lie, though she had no idea why she should. Only, Detective Megham's question sounded way too much like Geoffrey's had last night. It was one thing for a Pierce to think David might be involved in anything as abhorrent as frightening her and Claire half to death. It was another thing entirely for a police detective to be trying to tie him to a would-be attack and possibly a murder.

"I know him well enough to know that it wasn't him that Claire and I encountered last night."

"You just told me you didn't get a good look at the man, that all you saw was his outline in the shadows. The facial features were totally indistinguishable. That is what you said, isn't it?"

"Yes."

"Okay, I guess that's all for now, though I may have

some more questions later. In the meantime, I suggest you not go out alone after dark.''

"Surely you don't expect the man to come looking for me.''

"I'm not ruling out anything at this point." He stood and walked toward the front door. "And I'd definitely stay away from David Bryson.''

"He's not the man you're looking for.''

"I may know a lot more about that than you do. So take my advice. Stay away from him." With that he pushed through the door and stepped onto the porch.

She walked to the window and watched the detective saunter down the steps and climb into his car. He was only doing his job, trying to protect her and the other citizens of Moriah's Landing. Yet she disliked him immensely, beyond all reasonable explanation.

He was out to get David Bryson, to pin a murder on him that she knew David could never have committed. She had to warn him. No matter what had happened between them this morning, or maybe because of what had happened, she couldn't let him just fall into Megham's trap.

But what if she was wrong? What if she only saw in David what she wanted to see, let her fascination for the strange recluse from the castle on the hill color her judgment? What if her infatuation was leading her into the very kind of situation Detective Megham had just warned her about?

She knew nothing about David Bryson except that he was strange and moody and that he spent most of his life shut off from the rest of the world. All she really knew of herself right now was that she was infatuated with a man who seemed to hold strange powers over her. If there was such a thing as warlocks and magic, then he might well possess all the abilities that would bestow on him.

But he was not a killer. She'd stake her life on that. Even if it meant going back to the Bluffs to warn him that he might be the number-one murder suspect.

Go back to the Bluffs and face David again. Face him and then walk away. Walk away—if she could. Or else stay in his arms, locked away in a world of darkness and passion forevermore.

Chapter Seven

Not many bars were open on a Sunday night. Wheels was the exception, and it was doing a booming business on this particular evening. The customers were mostly bikers or fishermen and guys who sold bait or tackle along the wharves, but there were always a few guys from town who came down to drink and swap stories over a plate of onion rings and a burger.

Still, it wouldn't have been Becca's choice of a place to meet Larry. But since she was the one asking a favor, she didn't balk at his suggestion.

Larry leaned against the front bumper of his car while Becca climbed behind the wheel. "So where are you going on this mystery trip?" he asked.

"It's not a mystery. I told you. I just want to get away for a while, take a drive up the coast."

"I don't know why. It's practically dark now."

"I can still catch the sunset. Besides, I just need to get out of the house for a while."

"Yeah. I guess it's pretty depressing to watch Claire sliding back into the black hole she was in after the abduction."

"It is when there's nothing I can do to help. Worse,

I almost feel to blame. I was the one who asked her to dinner, and I was right there when she fell apart.''

"No one blames you. You were just lucky Geoffrey Pierce happened by when he did. Otherwise you might be…'' He pushed a faded baseball cap back on his head. "I don't even want to think about it. I don't feel great about your going off on your own tonight, either.''

"I'll be fine. I'll be in the car and I'll keep the doors locked.''

"I'd still feel better if you'd let me drive you. I could concentrate on the road. You could enjoy the sunset.''

"I appreciate the offer. I really do, but I just need time to think and I'll do that better if I'm by myself. I'll take good care of your car, and I'll be careful.''

"I'm not worried about the car. You know that. You've driven it before.'' He stepped over and closed her door. "Just don't stop in any isolated spots to catch the sunset. And stay away from Old Mountain Road. For all we know the knife-wielding maniac might still be hanging around there somewhere.''

"I won't go near it,'' she lied, not for the first time during this conversation. But if she told Larry the truth about why she needed to borrow his car and where she was going, he'd go ape on her. "I won't be more than a couple of hours at the most.''

"Then just pick me up back here at the bar. I'm gonna meet a couple of friends and grab a burger and a few beers.''

She turned the key in the ignition and the late-model Toyota hummed to life. Larry gave a wave and she waved back before backing out of the bar's parking lot and heading past the row of clapboard buildings and the clusters of weathered fishermen who hung out near the boats even when they weren't getting ready to go after the big ones.

The air smelled of fish and burgers, grease and salt water. Usually she liked it. It made her feel part of the community she'd chosen as home. Today it made her slightly nauseous, but she knew it was her nerves and not the odors that turned her insides to the consistency of curdled cream. She had no idea what kind of welcome she'd receive when she stood beneath the threatening gargoyles and knocked on the heavy wooden door of the Bluffs.

She'd tried to call David, but his number was unlisted. With her first choice of action aborted, she'd moved to the next, then gone back and forth with herself all afternoon. Going to the Bluffs meant facing David again, and after the roller coaster of emotions she'd experienced this morning, she wasn't sure she was up to that.

Still, here she was, driving the road to the Bluffs, apprehensive yet excited. The bittersweet truth was that she had never felt this way about any man before. Breathless and giddy and starved for his touch—as if she'd been waiting for him all her life without even knowing he existed.

She lowered the window and hoped the sting of the wind in her face would shock some sense into her before she reached the Bluffs. She might be a fool where David was concerned, but she didn't have to let him know it.

It was almost twilight when she turned onto Old Mountain Road. The trees cast deep pockets of shade over the winding, narrow road, and she felt as if she were suddenly cut off from the rest of the world. There were at least a half-dozen families who lived up this way, but the only sign of them were the occasional mailboxes at the side of the road beside dirt drives that disappeared into a seemingly impenetrable forest.

A cold shudder rumbled through her body as she neared the spot where the newspaper reported the body had been found. Had the victim already been dead when the killer brought her here or had she been pleading with him not to kill her? If she was alive, the feeling of isolation Becca felt now must have added to the horror and desperation.

She slowed as the road curved sharply and began the steady climb to the top of the cliff and the turnoff to the private road that led to David's fortress. She could see the roofline now, the turrets, the bulwarks, the battlements. Nothing was missing except a moat and a couple of fire-breathing dragons.

She caught a glimpse of a car in her rearview mirror. It was nice to know she wasn't totally alone out here—only the car was coming much too fast. No one should be driving this road at that speed. One missed curve and the car and driver would go hurtling over the cliff and onto the rocks far below. She slowed and moved far to the inside, giving him plenty of room to pass as they reached the one lone straight stretch in the road. Instead, he slowed as well, keeping the same distance between them.

Saliva pooled in her mouth and the muscles of her stomach and abdomen tightened. Peering through the rearview mirror, she tried to identify the driver, but the shadows on the road had deepened to an opaque blur and all she could see clearly was the car itself. Dark, either black or navy. A nondescript compact.

She lowered her foot on the accelerator, speeded up another five miles an hour. He did the same, staying exactly the same distance behind her.

Stay away from Old Mountain Road. Larry's warning echoed in her mind, but it was too late now. She was here. A split second later she felt a jolting impact. Her tires rumbled in the soft dirt on the side of the road, and she gripped the wheel with white knuckles, trying to steer the car back onto the road. It skidded across the center for terrifying seconds before she managed to get it back on course.

The driver had intentionally bumped her, and he was right behind her. The crazy fool was going to ram her again. Only this time he had moved to the inside. If he got a solid hit, she could spin totally out of control and toward the treacherous drop-off. It would be her, not him, who plunged to her death.

She toed the accelerator to the floor, but too late. Her body jerked, and the seat belt dug into her flesh as the other driver made a direct hit against her back fender. The car spun out of control, but miraculously she managed to straighten it and keep it going in the right direction.

The other car was on the inside now, between her and the protecting embankment. Finally, she could see the man's face, a skeletal frame with bits of brain and blood oozing from the yellowed bone.

She screamed, still clutching the steering wheel as he rammed her again, a solid hit that sent the car careening across the road. The air bags exploded into an expanding, choking pillow and all she could see was a cloud of white as the wheels of her car left the pavement and went flying into space.

All white. And then all black. The last thing she remembered was the hideous, decaying face of McFarland Leary, grinning at her as he sent her to her death.

Chapter Eight

David loosed his hold on the reins, giving Socrates free-dom to pick his own speed as they headed back toward his stables. The horse broke into a gallop, as if he knew they were going home.

Home. The word meant so little to David now. Nothing more than imprisoning walls and loneliness and a place to do his research. All the hopes and dreams he'd had when he bought the Bluffs destroyed in one unholy night five years ago.

It had been ludicrous for him to even imagine that it could change, that he could bring Becca there and that she would transform the house, bring laughter and life back into the musty, dark rooms of the aging mansion. It was past time he got over his preoccupation with her, anyway.

His heart would always belong to Tasha. His traitorous body was all he had left, a body still racked by desire though it was senseless to believe Becca or any other woman could want his hideous, deformed body. He mustn't ever let himself forget that.

But he had forgotten. He'd kissed Becca and almost forgotten everything. Instinctively he touched the fingers of his right hand to his lips. He could still taste her. Tart, sweet, berries and champagne.

A deafening crash of metal on metal reverberated through the night air, thrusting him back to reality. Socrates bolted, then skidded to a stop, almost catapulting David into a cluster of brush. A horn was going off, as well, a piercing, earsplitting blaring that wouldn't quit.

He jerked the reins to the left and urged Socrates toward the source of the clamor. Some dupe driving too fast, probably swerved into the opposite lane when rounding a curve. They'd had a fatality from that just over a year ago. Hopefully, this one wasn't that serious.

The path to the road was steep and thick with undergrowth. Movement was slow, and the sun had disappeared below the horizon, bathing the area in the deep gray of twilight by the time he and his horse neared the road. Socrates picked his way down the last rocky ledge, finally clearing the heavy growth of trees and coming out along a stretch of curved embankment.

David craned his neck and searched for some sign of the wreck. At least one of the cars had to be around here somewhere. The horn was still blasting away, a piercing, penetrating alarm that echoed off the rocks and came to him in deafening stereo.

It wasn't until they were actually on the shoulder of the road that he spotted the tire marks, black, sliding almost sideways across the road and toward the edge of the cliff. If one of the cars, or both, had gone over the embankment, there was little chance for survivors.

He climbed from the horse's back and cautiously led Socrates across the road for a better look. Straining to see through the trees in the dim lighting, he scanned the area at the foot of the cliff. All he saw was the splash of the water slamming against the rocks. He walked to the left, around a young cedar, and finally he caught a glimpse of red metal. Not at the foot of the cliff, but miraculously wedged between the trunks of two spindly pine trees forty yards below him. The last possible barrier between solid ground and the rocks below.

The headlights were on, the horn blasting away, but there was no sign of movement. He tied Socrates to a tree and took off, half running, half sliding down the embankment.

His breathing was sharp and jagged, his bum leg aching by the time he reached the site. Grabbing a penlight from his pocket, he fell against the car and yanked the passenger door open, dreading what he might find. He saw the hair first, bathed in his small circle of light, spread like a golden halo over the head that was slumped against the steering wheel. He recognized her at once and his heart seemed to explode in his chest. Not Becca. Not like this.

He touched his hand to her blood-stained sweater. She didn't move, and he willed his mind and body not to collapse completely. His hand flew to the pulse spot in her neck. Strong. Steady. Relief flooded him, leaving him weak, but his gaze took in everything at once, looking for excessive bleeding, for a head wound, for an obvious fracture.

Becca raised her head and stared at him, blankly for a minute, as if she couldn't make him come into focus. "David. How did you get here?" She pushed away from the steering wheel and pushed a clump of bloody hair from her face.

"Don't try to move. Just tell me what hurts."

"My ears." She covered them with the palms of her hands. "Can you please turn that damn horn off?"

Relief was so sudden, so overwhelming, he burst into

laughter. The sound of it surprised him. He'd totally forgotten the feeling and the sound of his own laughter. He checked the bloody wound on her forehead and assured himself it was minor before he left her to stop the persistent bellowing.

It was his first real look at the damage to the car. The hood was crushed, apparently from the impact with the tree. From the looks of the tracks, the car had taken a zigzag course down the embankment, hit the first tree, then spun around and wedged itself in tight between the two of them. The back right bumper and passenger side door were also crushed. It wasn't evident what had happened to them.

It took a few minutes of straining and prying before he managed to get to the horn connection beneath the hood and dislodge it. By the time he finished, Becca was climbing out of the car. He rushed back and steadied her in his arms. "Where do you think you're going?"

"To check the damage to the car."

"First we need to check the damage to you."

"You don't understand. This isn't my car."

"It doesn't matter whose car it is, the damage is not going to get any worse while the car sits here. Lean against the car and let me have a look at you."

"I'm fine." She shoved her hair back from her face, then stared at the sticky red blood that clung to her fingers. "Except for this." She smeared the blood on the legs of her jeans. "I must have hit my head. It doesn't hurt, though."

"It's fairly superficial, more of a blunt blow, so you probably won't require stitches." He gave her a cursory examination, the best he could manage under the circumstances. She lifted her feet and arms and moved as he directed. "I don't see any sign of broken bones, but you have some scratches and cuts on your neck and along your right cheek. They may be from flying glass. The windshield is busted.''

"A few cuts and scratches. I'll take those. A few minutes ago, I thought I might be about to make my appearance at the Pearly Gates."

"You almost did.'' And the miracle of it all hit him again, somewhere deep inside him where he'd thought nothing existed except the horrible vacuum of loss. ''From what I can tell, you are in amazing shape for a woman who just missed going over the cliff.''

"Does that mean you're through poking and prodding?"

"I'm a doctor. Making patients miserable is what we do best.''

"I didn't think you were the kind of doctor who worked with patients?"

"I specialized in research, but that was after I got my medical degree and after I practiced for three years in family medicine."

"Then I'm in good hands.''

"Not good enough. You need to be checked over in the hospital. Do you have a phone in this car?"

"Who are you going to call?"

"An ambulance.''

"Then there's no phone.''

"Don't be ridiculous. You need a thorough checkup and X rays.''

"No, I need to…'' She moaned and stretched so that she had a better look at the front half of the car. ''Oh, God. Don't worry about an ambulance. I'll need a hearse after Larry sees his car.''

"I'm sure Larry will just be happy to know you're safe.''

"Right. Then he'll kill me."

Larry Gayle. David knew exactly who she was talking about. He was the guy she was with the other night when he'd talked to her outside Wheels, and he'd spotted them together on several occasions before that. He'd hated the sight of them walking and laughing together, having dinner, talking to friends. But she hadn't been with Larry tonight. She'd been driving the road alone.

"What were you doing out this way?"

"It's a long story. I don't want to get into it right now." She turned around, as if she were looking for someone or something, then wrapped her arms around her chest and shivered. "Can we just get out of here now? Do you have a car or something?"

"No. I was on Socrates."

"Socrates?"

"My horse. He's tied to a tree just up the hill. I can call Richard and get him to meet us here. He can drive you to the hospital." He would like to take her himself, make sure they gave her a complete examination, that they were gentle and thorough and...

And he was thinking the impossible. He wasn't going to walk in that hospital and face the life he'd left behind long ago. Even if he did, it wouldn't help Becca. If anything, it would work against her, make people hate her just because she was with him. Perhaps that was happening already.

"What happened out here, Becca?"

"I'll tell you everything later, but right now I just want to get out of here." She leaned against him. "But I'm not going to the hospital."

"I can't let him just drive you home. You need to be observed by medical professionals, at least for tonight." Even as he said the words, he knew what he would do.

"Just relax, Becca. I'll call Richard. You'll be safe and cared for. I'll see to that."

He circled her waist with his arms and pulled her close. Her hair brushed against his cheek. He shouldn't take her home with him, but he would. He couldn't help himself. He was lost in a need he didn't understand at all.

CIGARETTE SMOKE HOVERED just below the low ceiling of Wheels, like smog with no place to go. A country tune from the jukebox played in the background, and in the rear of the bar, a shaggy-haired man and a peroxide blonde old enough to be his mother were dancing cheek to cheek. When the boats came in the party began, and everyone was invited. Larry wasn't sharing in the spirit of celebration.

He nursed his beer and tried to follow Kevin Pinelle's banter. The guy was a talker, but he never said anything that amounted to a mouthful, and right now he was really starting to get on Larry's nerves. "Gee, man, don't you ever just sit quietly?"

"Sure. When I'm home, and if you don't like talking, that's where you should be. But don't take it out on me 'cause your woman ran out on you. I don't know why you're fretting, anyway. I've never met a woman who wasn't replaceable. I say we go talk to the two who just came in." He nodded toward a table by the side wall.

Larry gave the girls a once-over, and one of them flashed him a come-on smile. "Not my type," he said, though on another night he might have settled. He pushed up the sleeve of his plaid flannel shirt and stared at his watch. Becca was an hour overdue and not a word from her. It wasn't like her, and he couldn't help wondering where she was and why she'd been so insistent that she go alone tonight.

"They sure look like my type," Kevin said, still staring at the women.

"Yeah. They're breathing. You go ahead. I've seen you in action. You can handle two babes without my help."

"That I can, my man." He smiled and tipped his beer bottle in the ladies' direction. They smiled back. "But you might as well join me. Hell, if you can't be with the one you love, love the one you're with. One or two—or more, if you're lucky."

"One's plenty for me."

"So are you hung up on Becca Smith?"

"Could be."

"Big mistake, my friend. The trick is to have them hung up on you. Besides, I hear Becca's making visits to the castle on the hill. Personally I wouldn't want any part of my body to come in contact with a woman who'd been touched by that freak."

"Crap, Kevin. She went up there on a job. If he touched her at all, it was to shake her hand."

"Don't kid yourself. David Bryson may look and act like something from a sideshow, but he's a man like the rest of us. If he's having a looker like Becca up to Frankenstein Manor, he's either doing her already or he's planning on making a move on her."

"Where'd you get that idea?"

"What idea? That the freaking beast has the hots for Becca? You figure it out. He sits up there all day by himself, then comes to town at night and sneaks around in the shadows like some bloodthirsty vampire. And he's singled Becca Smith out. He sent his driver to pick her up yesterday and she stayed up there half the day."

"I told you. That was all business."

"Oh, yeah, ri-i-ight. You are a sucker, my friend. She's probably up there with him now, in your car. And you're sitting here worried about her while two good-looking babes go lonely."

"Becca is not with David Bryson. That much I can promise you. I'll wait for her. The chicks are all yours."

"They will be. Watch. You might learn something." He stood, raked his fingers through his hair, mussing it instead of straightening it, then sauntered over to the table and joined the two women. They were hot-looking, both wearing sweaters that were at least a size too small. Their nipples were perfectly outlined, leaving little to the imagination. Another time he'd have liked to join Kevin, but not tonight.

Not that he put any stock in Kevin's opinions. The guy just loved to stir up trouble. But if he did find out that Becca had taken his car to visit David...

The bartender stopped in front of him and pushed a portable phone across the counter. "It's for you. Keep it short. This is a business and that is a business phone."

Larry pressed the phone to his ear to hear above the din of the bar. "Hello."

"Is this Larry Gayle?"

"Yes. Who's this?"

"David Bryson. There's been an accident."

"What kind of accident?"

"Becca ran your car off the road. She's fine, but the car can't be driven as it is."

"How do you know about this?"

"I happened on the accident right after it happened."

"Wasn't that convenient."

"It was for Becca."

"Where was the wreck?"

"On Old Mountain Road, but I've taken the liberty of calling a tow truck. They're hauling it to Grange's Garage, probably as we speak."

Old Mountain Road. The one place Becca had said she'd stay away from—the road to David's stone monstrosity. Larry fought the urge to slam his fist into something—into anything since David's face wasn't close enough to take the blow.

"And suppose I don't want it taken to Grange's Garage?"

"Then call them and have them take it wherever you like. I'll take care of any charges your insurance doesn't cover."

Big man. He'd take care of everything, just like he had with Tasha Pierce. "I don't need your stinking charity. Where's Becca?"

"She's here with me."

"Well isn't that just a full net of flounder. You tell her I'll borrow a car and be there to pick her up in half an hour."

"That won't be necessary. I'll have my butler drive her home."

"Let me talk to her."

"It would be better if you didn't, at least not until you calm down. She's had a rough couple of hours, and she's resting now."

"Resting, is she? In a house with a ghoul? Now, that would be enough to give any woman nightmares."

Larry broke the connection and slammed the phone onto the counter. Picking up what was left of his beer, he downed it in one continuous gulp. Five years ago he'd been dating Tasha Pierce when she dropped him like a smelly mackerel and joined up with David Bryson.

But then David hadn't looked like a monster. Now he

did. And still Becca Smith had gone running up to see him tonight, even after she'd been warned. The man had strange powers over women. Larry had never believed in the tales of witches, warlocks and ghosts that half the town did, but David Bryson was not human.

He was certain of it. And he had been allowed to live much too long. It was time someone did something about that. And past time someone taught Becca Smith a real lesson, one she wouldn't forget.

BECCA STRETCHED OUT on the sofa in the drawing room and propped her feet on a tufted, antique hassock. David had built a fire when they'd come in and Richard had served her tea and fresh scones topped with lemon curd, a custom he'd apparently brought over with him from England. Now she was alone in a room illuminated only by the flames that darted and danced in the mammoth fireplace.

"Everything's taken care of," David announced as he stepped back into the room. "I reported the hit-and-run to the police but told them you weren't up to talking just yet. They didn't like it but agreed to wait until morning to get your version of the wreck. Then I called for a tow truck and got in touch with Larry Gayle. He was still at the bar just as you thought he might be."

"Was he furious?"

"That's a pretty apt description of his mood."

"He'll probably never speak to me again."

"Actually, I had to persuade him not to come running to your rescue. He's afraid for you to be in a house with a ghoul. I think that's how he put it."

"Oh, David, I'm sorry."

"No need to be. He's probably right." He walked over and settled in a chair in the corner. "If you feel like talking, I'd like to hear the full story of what happened this evening.''

She stared into the fire, watched a log break and tumble off the grate, setting off a crackling spray of yellow flames. "I guess I should start at the beginning." She ran her hands across the rough denim of her jeans, trying to ease the clamminess. "Detective Megham made another visit to the Cavendish home this afternoon."

"Does he have any leads on the man who tried to attack you and Claire?"

"He thinks he does." She turned to face him and as always felt the heat of awareness shimmy through her. She wished there was a better way to say this. "He thinks it could be you."

"Did he say that?"

"Not exactly, but he intimated not only that it was you last night but that you're the man who murdered the woman whose body was found two nights ago."

David's expression and voice remained calm. "When in need of a suspect, go for the monster on the hill, the one man in town who doesn't dance to the Pierces' tune."

"I don't think this has anything to do with the Pierces."

"Then you have a lot to learn about living in Moriah's Landing. Everything that goes on in this town has to do with the Pierces. What else did the good detective say?"

"That I should stay away from you, that you're dangerous."

"Yet here you are."

"I thought you should know what was going on."

"So you borrowed Larry's car and were on your way to see me when some kook plowed into you and just kept going."

"It wasn't exactly hit-and-run."

"Exactly what was it, Becca?"

"The crash wasn't an accident. I was intentionally run off the road. The driver of the other car jammed into me repeatedly until I lost control of the car."

"Damn." David stood, walked to the hearth and leaned against the mantel.

"Did you see the driver of the other car?"

"I saw what looked like McFarland Leary."

David crossed the room in long strides and sat down beside her, careful to keep his right side turned away from her. "What are you talking about?"

"Just before the car hit me for the last time, I got a quick look at the driver. At the time, I thought I was glimpsing hell itself. But I'm sure now it was just a man wearing one of those rubber McFarland Leary masks that are in all the tourist shops."

"You could have been killed by an idiot in a mask," he said, his voice cracking. He put an arm around her shoulder and pulled her so close she could feel the beating of his heart against her breasts.

And then he kissed her, not the feather-soft whisper of a kiss that they'd shared that morning, but a deep, ravenous kiss that tore her apart and then put her back together again, more whole than she'd ever been. He kissed her again and again until her lips were swollen and tender and still she couldn't bear to pull away.

Finally he did, but he cradled her face in his hands, and when her gaze met his, it was as if he were still kissing her. "I shouldn't have done that, Becca. I had no right, not after what you've been through."

"It wasn't just you who did it. No kiss could be like that if only one person was involved. Surely you know that."

"I'm not sure what I know right now." He covered the right side of his face with his hand as he drew away, as if suddenly aware that he'd let her glimpse too much of his deformity.

Strange that it should bother him so much when it was no more than a shadowy illusion in the firelight. She wasn't sure that it would have mattered, anyway. It was not so much what she saw when she looked at him but what she felt that consumed her.

"I'll have Richard ready the guest room. We'll talk again in the morning."

"I need to call Mrs. Cavendish and let her know I won't be back tonight. After that, will you sit with me for a while, stay with me until I fall asleep?"

"If you want me to."

"I do." Wanted him in a way that defied all reason. Wanted him no matter what the cost.

THE WIND BLEW ACROSS the cemetery, stirring the dry leaves and tossing them around like the old dreams of people who were buried there. So many graves. Yet only one mausoleum held any fascination for the lone man strolling through the maze of tombstones and dead bouquets.

Five years ago he'd abducted Claire Cavendish from that spot. She had been the perfect victim. Young, beautiful, fragile. That's why he'd weakened, kept her alive for days while he played sick games with her body and her mind. But keeping her alive had turned out to be the worst mistake of his life. She'd escaped before he could silence her forever.

Somewhere in the scarred corners of her mind, she knew who he was. Knew his name and the sound of his voice. And one day she'd walk back into those dark chambers and the veil would lift. As long as she'd stayed locked away in that hospital, he hadn't worried much. Who'd believe a crazy person if she pulled a name from her memory and claimed he'd ravaged her body and soul?

But now she was out, making progress, walking the streets, talking to people, especially to Becca Smith. He had to kill Claire. That was the only way to make sure his gruesome secrets stayed locked away. He'd kill her and he'd kill Becca Smith.

He'd already tried this afternoon, but his plan hadn't worked. Dear old David Bryson had come to her rescue. But he would kill both women before this was over.

He'd kill Claire because he had no alternative. He'd kill Becca because she was consorting with a madman.

And for the pure thrill of it.

He'd do it soon. He had to. The need to kill was taking over his mind the way it always did. And when it became too loud to silence, he had no choice but to spill the bright red blood of a beautiful woman like Becca Smith.

Chapter Nine

David paced the hall outside the guest room where Becca slept, his footsteps the only noise in the eerily silent house. They seemed to echo in his ears, like warning drums, while visions of Becca danced in his head. Just as he'd promised, he'd sat beside her bed until she'd fallen asleep.

Lying there in one of *his* T-shirts, the soft cotton draping the gentle curves of her breasts, her silken hair fanned across the creamy sheen of the pillowcase, catching the soft rays of moonlight that filtered through the window.

He was still reeling from the effect. His feelings for her were frighteningly strong, consuming, and yet so different from the love he'd felt for Tasha. With Tasha, everything had been right from the very beginning, as if the second they met, they knew they were meant to be together.

With Becca, everything was wrong except the ridiculously overwhelming attraction that made him seek her out over and over until he'd finally weakened and pulled her into the shadowy, empty shell of life he inhabited.

Tasha had made him strong. Becca made him vulnerable. But she needed his protection. He hadn't been sure last night's attack had been directed at her specifically, but there was no doubt about today's. Someone wanted her dead, and he wouldn't stand by and watch her get killed, the way he had with Tasha. She would have to listen to reason now, agree to stay at the Bluffs where he could make certain she was safe.

Only how could he have her here day after day and not touch her? How could he look into her eyes and not want to kiss her? How could he bear going to bed night after night alone when she was asleep in the same house?

"David."

The voice was high-pitched, a cry for help. It cut through him, fueling a rush of adrenaline. He pushed through the door of the guest room, expecting to see Becca sitting up in bed, fighting off the dregs of a nightmare. Instead, she was still in its clutches. Her eyes were closed, and she was writhing, twisting from side to side, tangling her body and legs in the sheets. Scared to death even in her sleep.

He sat down beside her and lay a hand to her shoulder. "I'm here, Becca. I'm right here. You're safe."

The twitching stopped and her breath slowed to a steady pace. She reached up and placed her hand over his, and a surge of desire shot through him with dizzying force. His fingers dug into her flesh, the smoothness of her like silk against the rough flesh of his hands.

She stirred again, this time opening her eyes. "David?" Her voice was hoarse, as if she'd been screaming for hours instead of calling for him once.

"I'm right here."

She rubbed her eyes with the heels of her hands, then looked around the room, her eyes narrowed, as if trying to see through a dense fog. She wet her dry lips with the tip of her tongue and then turned her gaze to him, the moonlight painting surreal shadows on her face. She tried to roll to her side and winced in pain, before giving up.

"You're in pain."

"A little."

"Show me exactly where it hurts."

"Yes, Doctor." She was teasing him, but she touched her hand to a spot on her right side just below her waist. "Here."

Making sure the right side of his face was turned away from her, he flicked the bedside lamp on low. Gingerly, he lifted the shirt, leaving the sheet high enough that he didn't see any more of her body than was necessary.

"You have an ugly bruise. It looks as if the catch on the seat belt may have dug into your flesh when you stopped."

"I think I even remember that. See. Nothing to worry about."

"Any other sharp pains or areas that seem overly sensitive?"

"My neck and shoulders are stiff. Kind of a dull ache, no worse than I get after a day of nonstop sewing."

"Let me see you sit up."

"Aw, c'mon, Doc. We did all this already." But she rose to her elbows and then pushed herself to a sitting position. "See. I'm up. Back straight. Chest out."

His gaze went to her chest, which was most assuredly out. She was joking and teasing, trying to keep the moment light. He didn't even remember how to joke and flirt. But then he'd thought he didn't remember how to feel the needs and the urges that were currently driving him over the edge, either. He'd been wrong.

Struggling for a steady hand and a reasonably clear mind, he switched off the lamp, then concentrated on the pillows, plumping them and propping them behind her back.

She leaned back and sighed contentedly, though he was certain she was working hard to keep from showing the stiffness of her muscles. "You have a terrific bedside manner," she said, smoothing the sheet.

"Thank you, but I'm not sure the medical ethics board would approve of my bringing the patient home with me to treat her."

"I wasn't your patient. I was an accident victim, and you were merely fulfilling your Hippocratic oath by taking me in."

He doubted Hippocrates would see it that way, and he was certain Larry Gayle didn't. He had a strong suspicion that Mrs. Cavendish hadn't, either, though he'd only heard Becca's end of the conversation when she'd called to tell her she was spending the night with him.

Becca stretched, letting her toes slide down the underside of the sheet. "When was the last time someone slept in this bed?"

"Years ago."

"You should open the Bluffs to company again. The place has character and history—and room. Definitely room. I'm glad this is one of the rooms you're planning to redecorate. It cries for burgundy, don't you think?"

"I don't hear any crying." And if he did, it would be his own, crying in desperation because he was playing a game he could never win. She stared at him, critically, as if she were trying hard to read his mind, her fingers massaging a spot at the base of her skull.

"Let me do that for you," he said. "Then I'll give you something to help you relax and get back to sleep."

She shook her head. "I don't take drugs unless I absolutely have to."

"Good, because I don't have any painkillers on hand stronger than an aspirin. I was thinking about a little sherry."

"Sherry I can handle."

He scooted closer so that he could fit his hands around the curve of her neck. She turned away from him to make the task easier. His fingers trailed the taut lines, from her earlobes to the curl of her shoulders, gently at first, to let her adjust to his touch.

Slowly he increased the pressure, circling her shoulders with his thumbs, then working his way up her neck, thoroughly, until he felt the kinks begin to release. She rolled her neck, and silky locks of her golden hair slid over his fingers and hands. His body hardened, and instinctively he jerked away.

She turned and stared at him, her usually bright blue eyes smoky and seductive. "Why did you stop?"

He hesitated. "I thought you were ready for the sherry."

"The sherry?" She touched two fingers to his lips, and traced the outline of them.

He parted his lips and she slipped her fingers between them, the movement so erotic he lost the battle for control. He sucked and nibbled her fingers, his body reacting as if it were a separate entity, as if all he could do was go along for the ride and accept his destiny.

He wasn't sure who made the first move, or maybe they did it together. All he knew was that their lips met. He kissed her over and over again—couldn't stop, didn't want to stop. He let his mind go numb and his feelings take over. He felt the heat of her beneath the cotton shirt, reeled from urges that possessed his body, ached to make love to her the way a man should make love to a woman.

Nothing held back. Just give and take, and drown in the pleasure.

Her hands were all over him. In his hair, trailing his rib cage, dancing along his waist. Moving lower, searing a path toward his abdomen. Touching the spot—

Reality surfaced in an eye-opening blow of frustration as her hands paused over the grotesque patch of blotchy, wrinkled flesh that darkened his belly. He'd lost his mind completely, giving in twice in one night to this crazy, destructive hunger. He couldn't have her, not now and not ever. Once she saw him, she'd run away in disgust.

"I'm sorry, Becca."

She held out her hands, palms up, her eyes flashing. "Why do you keep doing this? You kiss me senseless and then withdraw and say you're sorry as if you've stepped on my toe."

He backed away from the bed. "You're intrigued by a legend, by some beast who lives in a forbidden castle on the hill."

"Maybe I was at first, but not now. Not since I've met you."

"But you haven't met me, not really. I'm *not* just a legend, Becca. I am a beast, a hideously ugly beast who's best left to hide in shadows and dark chambers."

"Give me a chance, David. Let me see you—not in the shadows, but in the light."

He stood and thrust his hands into the front pockets of his trousers. "I can't do that."

"So you can just pretend you didn't like kissing me just now and move on?"

"I never said this was the way I wanted it. It's the way it has to be."

"This morning you wanted me to move in with you. Now I feel as if you're kicking me out of your life."

"No. I want you here, at the Bluffs. You'll be safe here, even from me. Especially from me. I won't bother you again."

"You won't touch me and yet I know you want to. Are you sure it's because of your appearance? Or is it because you're still in love with Tasha Pierce?"

"My personal life is my business."

"Tasha's dead, David, and no amount of wishing she wasn't will ever bring her back."

Her words ground inside him, cutting and tearing at his heart. "This isn't about Tasha."

"Then what is it about?"

Damn, but he wished he knew the full answer to that, but the truth was snarled and convoluted, too tangled for him to unravel. It was part of the past and the present and the future that Becca might not have if she got mixed up with him. It was the fact that he was only a mangled scrap of a man—a sight too hideous for any woman to bear. And, on some level, it was still Tasha. It would always be Tasha.

So he did the cowardly thing, walked away without answering. It was the only choice he had, but as he walked the dark hallway to his own room, he felt the loss deep in his gut. There was no way out of the hell he lived in.

BECCA OPENED HER EYES to bright sunlight streaming across her bed and the odor of fresh perked coffee. And to Richard Crawford setting out china, silver and napkins on the round table next to the window. She stayed beneath the covers.

"Room service, and I didn't even order. I like this place better all the time."

"I hated to wake you, but a Detective Carson

Megham has already called three times this morning. Apparently he wants to talk with you about your accident. I've managed to put him off so far, but he seems determined on paying you a visit.''

"Jeez! There goes the neighborhood.''

"It sounds as if you know this detective.''

"For the last couple of days, I seem to see him more often than I do my toothbrush.'' Thinking of which, hers was back at the Cavendishes'. So was her hairbrush, and her hair was probably a mass of tangles. And she wasn't sure where her watch was, either. "What time is it?''

"Ten past ten.''

"You're kidding. I haven't slept this late in years. No wonder Megham's called three times.''

"Yes, ma'am. Dr. Bryson said you needed the sleep.''

"Evidently he was right, but still I'm surprised I didn't wake with the sun as I usually do.''

"You had no way of knowing the sun was up. It was dark as a cave in here before I tied back the curtains a minute ago. Can I pour you a cup of coffee, ma'am?''

"You can if you promise not to call me ma'am. Becca will do nicely. Do you always refer to David as Dr. Bryson?''

"Yes. I know it's too formal for the younger generation, but it was customary in the family where I worked before moving to America, and old habits die hard.''

He poured the coffee from an insulated pitcher into a china cup. "Cream and sugar?''

"Just black. Where is David this morning? Is he sleeping in, too?''

He arched his brows. "Hardly. He was up at seven and has been in his lab since before eight.''

"He must be working on a very important project.''

"He never talks with me about his work, but he puts

in lots of hours in the lab, so I'm sure it's important.'' Richard placed the coffee on the bedside table. ''I took the liberty of bringing you a scone and some marmalade. I thought you might be a bit hungry. There's a cup of fresh fruit as well. But the cook is here today, so if you want a full breakfast, I'm sure she can handle that.''

''You mean a scone with marmalade isn't a full breakfast?''

''Not to me.''

Finally she'd coaxed a smile to his face. He was a nice-looking man, and if he'd lived anywhere but the Bluffs, the local widows would be baking him pies and inviting him to church socials every chance they got.

Richard stepped away from the table and toward the door. ''Is there anything I can get you?''

Information, but she wasn't quite sure how to approach the subject, since he was obviously very protective of his boss. She decided on the questioning approach. ''Did David tell you about the wreck?''

''Do you mean the fact that it was intentional?''

''So he did tell you.''

''We discussed it briefly this morning.''

''Do you think I should stay at the Bluffs while I work on the redecorating project, Richard?''

''It doesn't really matter what I think. This isn't my house.''

''I'm interested in your opinion.''

''Your coming to the Bluffs Saturday upset a lot of people, Becca. Your spending the night here last night is going to upset a lot more. But I'm sure Dr. Bryson thinks you're the right person for the job. If not, he wouldn't have asked you. And if he's asked you to move into the Bluffs, I'm sure he has his reasons.''

GIFTS from the Heart

Play and you can get **2 FREE BOOKS** and a **SURPRISE GIFT!**

GIFTS from the Heart

Play Gifts from the Heart and get 2 FREE Books and a FREE Gift!

HOW TO PLAY:

1. With a coin, carefully scratch off the gold area at the right. Then check the claim chart to see what we have for you — **2 FREE BOOKS** and a **FREE GIFT** — **ALL YOURS FREE!**

2. Send back the card and you'll receive two brand-new Harlequin Intrigue® novels. These books have a cover price of $4.50 each in the U.S. and $5.25 each in Canada, but they are yours to keep absolutely free.

3. There's no catch. You're under no obligation to buy anything. We charge nothing —**ZERO** — for your first shipment. And you don't have to make any minimum number of purchases — not even one!

4. The fact is, thousands of readers enjoy receiving books by mail from the Harlequin Reader Service®. They enjoy the convenience of home delivery... they like getting the best new novels at discount prices, **BEFORE** they're available in stores...and they love their *Heart to Heart* subscriber newsletter featuring author news, horoscopes, recipes, book reviews and much more!

5. We hope that after receiving your free books you'll want to remain a subscriber. But the choice is yours — to continue or cancel, any time at all! So why not take us up on our invitation, with no risk of any kind. You'll be glad you did!

A surprise gift
FREE!
We can't tell you what it is... but we're sure you'll like it! A
FREE GIFT!

Visit us online at
www.eHarlequin.com

just for playing **GIFTS FROM THE HEART!**

NO COST! NO OBLIGATION TO BUY!
NO PURCHASE NECESSARY!

PLAY GIFTS from the Heart

Scratch off the gold area with a coin.
Then check below to see the gifts you get!

YES! I have scratched off the gold area. Please send me the 2 Free books and gift for which I qualify. I understand I am under no obligation to purchase any books as explained on the back and on the opposite page.

381 HDL DNL3   181 HDL DNLR

FIRST NAME	LAST NAME

ADDRESS

APT.#	CITY

STATE/PROV.   ZIP/POSTAL CODE

♥♥♥♥ 2 free books plus a surprise gift

♥♥♥ 2 free books   ♥♥ 1 free book

(H-I-05/02)

The Harlequin Reader Service® — Here's how it works:

Accepting your 2 free books and gift places you under no obligation to buy anything. You may keep the books and gift and return the shipping statement marked "cancel." If you do not cancel, about a month later we'll send you 4 additional books and bill you just $3.80 each in the U.S., or $4.21 each in Canada, plus 25¢ shipping & handling per book and applicable taxes if any.* That's the complete price and — compared to cover prices of $4.50 each in the U.S. and $5.25 each in Canada — it's quite a bargain! You may cancel at any time, but if you choose to continue, every month we'll send you 4 more books, which you may either purchase at the discount price or return to us and cancel your subscription.

*Terms and prices subject to change without notice. Sales tax applicable in N.Y. Canadian residents will be charged applicable provincial taxes and GST.

If offer card is missing write to: Harlequin Reader Service, 3010 Walden Ave., P.O. Box 1867, Buffalo NY 14240-1867

BUSINESS REPLY MAIL
FIRST-CLASS MAIL   PERMIT NO. 717-003   BUFFALO, NY

POSTAGE WILL BE PAID BY ADDRESSEE

HARLEQUIN READER SERVICE
3010 WALDEN AVE
PO BOX 1867
BUFFALO NY 14240-9952

NO POSTAGE
NECESSARY
IF MAILED
IN THE
UNITED STATES

"He hasn't done a very good job of explaining those reasons to me."

"Some men are afraid to admit what they want, even to themselves."

That response surprised her, but she knew it was a deliberate statement and not a slip of the tongue. Everything about Richard seemed deliberate. "Did you know Tasha Pierce?" she asked, then wondered why she'd bothered. She knew as much about Tasha as she needed to know. Knew she was perfect and wonderful and that David had never gotten over her.

"Yes. I had been working for David about six months when they met."

"They must have been very much in love."

"As in love as I've ever seen two people."

She stared out the window. She hated thinking about David and Tasha together, but the image stayed in her mind. A young David. Without scars and deformities. Without the brooding and mysterious eyes. "I guess a man falls in love like that only once in a lifetime."

"Love is infinite, Becca. Like the universe, the stars, the planets. It goes on and on forever. Every time it's different, but it can never be measured or compared."

A glimmer of something Becca didn't fully understand stirred inside her. It was warm like summer sun on the sand. "You are either a very wise man, Richard Crawford, or you have had a lot of experience with life."

"It's a combination, but keep it our secret." He winked. "In this town, having insight can get you labeled as a warlock, and I don't want the tour guides adding me to their list of strange local phenomena."

"Do you believe in people being bewitched, Richard?"

He looked at her, studied her as if trying to decide if

her question was serious before he answered. Instead he returned the question. "Do you?"

"I'm not sure. I was sure, but I just don't know what I believe anymore."

"It's this town that does that to you." He met her gaze, his eyes dark, troubled. "To answer your question, I don't believe in ghosts and witches, but there's a spirit of evil in Moriah's Landing that can't be explained rationally. And there's a presence in the Bluffs."

"What do you mean by a presence?"

"Cold spots and areas that make the hairs on your neck stand on end when you pass them late at night."

Just the description made hers stand on end. "Then you do believe in the supernatural."

"I believe there are powers beyond what mortals possess. Some good. Some bad."

She shuddered, unable to shake the chill that had overcome her.

"I'm sorry if I frightened you, Becca. This house is perfectly safe. I didn't mean to suggest that it wasn't. Now, I'm going to get out of here and let you drink your coffee and eat your scone. Then you should probably shower and get dressed. Detective Megham will be here at eleven-thirty. There are clean towels in the bathroom across the hall. A new toothbrush and toothpaste, too, and you'll find personal soaps and shampoos in the basket on the counter. If you need anything else, just let me know."

"I can't think of a thing." Except that she'd like to see David before the detective showed up. Unless she was mistaken, Megham had more than the accident in mind. That was why he was so anxious to talk to her while she was at the Bluffs. "I'd really like to talk to

David. Do you think he'd mind if I visited him in the lab after I'm dressed?''

"I know he'd mind. No one is allowed in the lab while he's working. Not even me.''

"Never?''

"Not in the five and a half years I've worked for him.''

"Will he be coming back to this part of the house when the detective comes?''

"I don't think that's his intention.''

"Will you take me home after the detective's visit?''

"I know that Dr. Bryson would prefer you stay here.''

"As a prisoner?''

"Of course not. If you insist on leaving, I'll drive you into town.''

"Were those David's orders?''

"They were his instructions.''

And so like David. They touched when he wanted it, kissed when he wanted it. And when he wanted out of her life, he merely walked away, buried himself in his lab where no one was allowed.

She'd be a fool to stay here on his terms, and yet, how could she carry the danger that followed her back into the Cavendish home? They had been through so much already.

Which left Becca with exactly nowhere to go. No significant other to run to, no mother who'd protect and love her the way Claire's mother did her, no family to shelter her. She'd be alone again.

RICHARD MANAGED TO HIDE his smile until he was out of sight of Becca Smith. He had the strange but comforting feeling that in spite of what she said, she wasn't going to run away. After five long years they might be about to have a woman in the house again. Not just any woman, but a beautiful lady who was smart and spunky and tough.

He'd almost frightened her off by telling her the truth about the Bluffs. He'd have to watch that in the future. She'd find out soon enough on her own.

Becca would bring youth and laughter back into the house, and with any luck at all she just might lead David back to the land of the living. Of course, she'd have to march right through Tasha's memory to do it. But if he was a wagering man, he'd put his money on Becca Smith.

How was it they said it over here? You go, girl. You go.

Chapter Ten

Becca couldn't remember when a shower had felt so good. The hot water pulsated into her sore shoulders and rolled down her back in welcome rivulets of moist heat. After a few minutes of soaking up the steam and relief, she turned so that the showerhead directed the full spray to the back of her neck. She'd probably be achy and stiff for days, but she was just thankful she could move without too much pain. She took that as an omen that there were no injuries that would require medical care.

Taking the fresh bar of soap from the holder, she rolled it over and over in the washcloth until she had a foamy lather to spread over her body. Bending slowly, she sucked up the pain and ran the rag over her legs. The right calf had a purple-and-black bruise, ugly, but not nearly as ugly as Larry's car had looked with the front of it crushed into an accordion.

She straightened and groaned again, not only from the pain that shot through her hip but from the prospect of having to face Larry. Hopefully she could put off the face-to-face encounter until tomorrow, but she'd have to call him today. She owed him an explanation of some kind.

First Megham, then Larry. And by that time David

might have surfaced from the forbidden lab. And those
were just the people supposedly on her side. Somewhere
out there was a man who'd tried to kill her.

Could life get any better than this?

CLAIRE STOOD AT THE WINDOW, her mind sliding in and
out of reality. One minute, she pictured Becca, locked
away in the haunted stone fortress that harbored death
and sordid powers from the underworld. The next, she
slid back in time, to a September night five years ago.

Fear, desperation, madness. They closed in on her,
choking her, making her weak. Trembling, she closed
her eyes as the familiar curse fell on her like rain from
a black cloud.

It was so dark in the mausoleum. She couldn't see
anything, but she could smell death all around her. Dank.
Clammy. Caustic. But she was young. Death couldn't
hurt her. All she had to do was stay in here for a few
minutes, and it would all be over.

She, Brie, Kat, Elizabeth, Tasha. They would have
passed the test, proved their worthiness for admission
into the most prestigious sorority at Heathrow. The others were right outside, waiting for her. She'd drawn the
picture of McFarland Leary, but any of them would have
taken her place if she'd let them. They were those kind
of friends, thoughtful and protective. One for all and all
for one.

She concentrated on the positive as she moved deeper
into the inner chambers of the tomb. It was colder here,
as if death were trying to reach out and pull her into its
clutches. Something started crawling up her leg beneath
her jeans. Panic knotted her insides. She shook and
kicked, but the creature clung tenaciously until she
trapped it between her jeans and her legs and crushed

its life away. Likely a spider, though it could have been anything with legs, and for all she knew the floor was alive with them.

Don't think about them. A few more steps. Make it all the way to the back. Then she could light her one match that the sorority allowed and retrieve the gold box that proved she had indeed visited the house of the dead.

Something flew by her head. She put up her hand to protect her eyes from what had to be a bat. She tripped and pitched forward, catching herself on a wall of cold, abrasive concrete. Thank God, she'd surely made it all the way to the back of the mausoleum. She reached in her pocket for the matchbox with the lone match inside it. Something clamped around her arm before she could, and a large, foul-smelling hand covered her mouth, trapping her scream inside her dry throat.

The sound of ragged breathing seemed to echo through the tomb, but she wasn't sure if it was hers or the person's who smelled of aftershave and whiskey. Fear roared in her brain, terror so excruciating she thought her heart was going to thrust itself through the walls of her chest.

She felt the sting of a needle as it punctured her flesh and sank deep into the veins in her arm. And then the pit opened and sucked her inside.

"No. No. No. No."

"Claire. It's all right, sweetie. I'm right here."

Claire's eyes flew open. She was incredibly cold—bone cold—as if her veins coursed with frigid blood. She fell into her mother's open arms and held on tight. If she didn't, she'd fall back into the pit.

Her mother rocked her to her breast, stroked her hair and her back. "Don't go back there, Claire. Don't go back to that horrible place in your mind where you get so frightened.''

''I can't help it. It just happens. I don't go looking for it, but it finds me and drags me back there.''

''Well, I won't let it have you. Not again. At least not for good. I'll always be here to pull you back to safety.''

''I'm counting on that.''

But she would go back, over and over, until her mind finally let her see past the pit, see the face of the man who'd abducted her that night and taken her to hell. That was the only thing that would ever free her from the terror—free her or destroy her completely.

''I'm okay now, Mama.''

''Are you sure, sweetie? I can stay right here with you. No one will notice if the kitchen goes unmopped.''

''No. Go ahead with what you were doing. I'll just lie down on the couch and rest a bit.''

''That's a good idea. You rest and I'll be back to check on you in a few minutes.''

Claire waited until her mother was out of hearing range before she picked up the phone and dialed Larry's number at work. She hated to bother him, but she knew he'd be as upset as she was about Becca's being seduced by David Bryson's evil powers. Larry was the one person she could count on to understand that there was no time to waste.

They had to save Becca before it was too late.

BECCA WOULD HAVE LOVED to have clean clothes to step into after her shower, but she had no choice. Tossing her wet towel over the rack, she slipped back into the same things she'd had on yesterday—all except for the blood-stained pullover. The colored shirt she'd worn under the sweater was faded and worn, but it would have to do. The jeans were fine, though still smeared with her blood. And the toothbrush Richard had provided was a godsend.

There was no hairbrush, but she made good use of the comb she'd had in her purse, working to untangle the mass of hair until it fell in smooth waves over her shoulders. That and a touch of the lip gloss that she always carried and she felt presentable enough for the detective. Once she was dressed she went back to the guest room, stared out the window until she was thoroughly bored—about five minutes—then decided to stroll through the house. She'd pretty much seen this part of the house on her walk through with David the other day, but there were countless other areas that she hadn't explored.

Pans banged and clattered in the kitchen, and the steady whir of a vacuum cleaner drifted from somewhere down the hall. The noise and activity level made the place seem much less intimidating than it had on her first visit, and Becca hesitated only a minute before heading down the carpeted hall.

The moldings were painted a dusty cream, or else they'd yellowed to that color over the years, and the wallpaper was a muted flower pattern. Antique brass sconces, probably original to the house, had been converted to electricity, each with a tiny bulb that gave off a shimmery glow that made lacy patterns of light and shadow to illuminate the long hallway. She stopped at the first closed door and hesitated only a minute before easing it open. After all, Richard had said to make herself at home.

Another guest room, she guessed, judging from the lack of any personal touches. The headboard of the bed was elaborately carved with angels cavorting among rolling clouds and the mattress was covered with a flow-ered quilt, the stitching meticulous. An antique secretary stood against one wall, and a china pitcher and bowl sat on a mahogany stand near the heavily draped window.

She could easily imagine the room having looked the same way for the last hundred or so years. It still boggled her mind that the house had been built stone by stone in the 1600s, and for most of that time, the house had stayed in the Pierce family. David had been the first man to break the continuity of ownership. For the first time, she began to understand why the Pierces were so bitter about his living in the house.

First the house, then Tasha. He had claimed two of their most precious possessions, and at least some of them had never forgiven him.

She closed the door behind her, walked past a few more doors and then opened another. Apparently this room had been used as a child's playroom at some point in time. An antique doll cradle sat in the center of the room, and resting inside was a delicate porcelain doll dressed in a white christening gown. An army of carved wooden soldiers marched across a brass-hinged chest and a stack of leather-covered classics lined a mahogany bookcase, with all the books at a child's eye level. Shaggy teddy bears sat in miniature chairs at a table graced with a child's china tea set, and a metal tricycle stood as if ready for a tyke to crawl aboard and take off.

Her favorite room, hands down, Becca decided as she closed the door and stepped away and continued down the carpeted path, her mind playing with the idea of raising children in house so large and rambling, you'd have a difficult time finding them if they ever decided they didn't want to be found. In fact, if she wasn't careful she could get lost herself, especially here where the hallway intersected with another, offering three options.

If she continued straight, the surroundings looked the same as the way she'd come, the same lighting, the same carpeting, a similar series of closed doors on either side of the hall. To the right, the hall was unlit, and worn carpet the color of old blood trailed off toward what appeared to be a dead end.

To the left was a staircase that led to the second floor. She hesitated and then started climbing the steps, slowly, serenaded by the creaking of old boards. With each step, she seemed to be leaving behind what little life and activity the Bluffs provided. Fear chased along her nerve endings, quick, frigid, a reminder that she was entering a vast area of isolation where she'd never been before.

All but one of the doors along the hallway were closed. She moved toward it, then stopped instantly. A draft rolled across her, and she turned slowly, looking for the source of the cold air. There didn't seem to be one.

Richard's words flashed through her mind. *Unexplained cool spots.* It was downright creepy, and if there hadn't been the one open door up ahead, she'd have rushed back to the main part of the house.

And that would be stupid, she told herself. The house was centuries old. There could be any number of logical reasons for the draft she felt. She just couldn't think of them right now, but she might, if she knew what was inside the room that she was standing near.

Fitting her hand around the polished brass doorknob, she twisted, expecting the door to open as it had with the other rooms she'd peeked inside. This time, the circle of brass didn't move. Neither did the door. A locked room. Not so unusual in a house this size, but she did wonder why this one was locked and all the others hadn't been. Who was David keeping out?

She glanced at her watch. Eleven-thirty. Detective Megham was running late or else he was already here and no one knew where to find her. Well, it wouldn't hurt him to wait a few minutes, and she did want to at least glance inside the room with the open door, though it meant walking almost the length of the hallway. She all but ran the last few yards.

Her breath caught, then released in a slow, steady sigh as she stepped inside the door and got her first glimpse of one of the most remarkable views she'd ever seen. The haze had been burned away by the sun, and the water in Raven's Cove was a dazzling shade of turquoise, the surface studded with glittering diamonds.

Best of all, the view wasn't sabotaged by trees or scrubby brush. She could see the rocks that jutted below the cliff, the water dancing along the rims of the hard, jagged edges before splashing back to the sea. There were a couple of sailboats out today, taking advantage of the calm and the Indian summer weather.

The view had her so spellbound that it was several minutes before she turned to scan the rest of the room. Obviously, she was in a library. Floor-to-ceiling bookshelves lined every wall and two large desks flanked the center of the room. Stepping over to the bookshelves, she scanned the titles. Book after book about serial killers and crime-scene investigations and murders.

Walking to the desk, she let her gaze drop to an open file. The name Joyce Telatia was printed in black ink along the tab. Joyce Telatia. The name was familiar, but it took her a minute to remember where she'd heard it before. When she did, a sinking sensation settled in her stomach.

Joyce had been the fourth young woman murdered twenty years ago, the third of the three whose killer had never been caught. Becca flipped open the file and picked up the first sheet of paper and read the scribbled notations under Joyce's name. Blond hair. Five feet six inches tall. Blue eyes. Small boned. A hundred and twenty pounds.

It had to be Joyce's description, but it could have been Becca's. Twenty years ago Joyce had been the victim, and just yesterday Becca had barely missed being run from the road and killed in a deliberate car crash. The night before that, she'd narrowly missed being attacked less than a block from her home.

"Are you looking for something?"

She jumped at the sound of David's voice, then let her gaze circle the room. Finally she located him, in the back corner of the room, away from the light, standing so that his whole right side was hidden from view by a huge brass statue.

"I didn't know you were in here. Why didn't you say something?"

"You're a long way from the guest room, Becca. Are you lost?"

"No." She wouldn't be intimidated or frightened by him. "Richard said I should make myself at home. I was doing that."

"So I noticed. Do you know who Joyce Telatia is?"

"The fourth murder victim from twenty years ago. But why are you so interested in her, David?"

"Everyone in Moriah's Landing is interested in the murders. Reliving the horror is our community pastime." He buried his hands deep in the pockets of his trousers. "I don't want to seem inhospitable, Becca, but this part of the Bluffs is off-limits. Not only this room, but this whole section of the house."

"Will it still be off-limits if I accept your invitation to live here?"

"It will always be off-limits. I'd like for you to forget the things you saw in here today, and I'll have to ask you not to come back into this room—ever."

Some people even believe David was the one who committed the murders twenty years ago.

Larry's words crept through her mind, and she had to hold on to the edge of the desk for support as a wave of nausea overtook her. Taking a deep breath, she forced herself to concentrate on the facts. David had lived in Moriah's Landing at the time of the murders, had first-hand access to everything that was going on. He'd even been questioned in the deaths, adequate reason for him to be interested enough in this murder to have collected the information surrounding it.

"I don't think I'd like to live in a house with so many secrets," she said, backing toward the door.

"All of us have secrets, even you."

"Hidden away in the dark corners of my mind, perhaps, but not locked inside rooms. And I'm not intentionally hiding my past. I just can't find it to claim it." Still, she backed toward the door. "It wouldn't help your case any if Detective Megham was to see the files or the books in this room."

"I wasn't planning on inviting him in. But I do want you to stay, Becca. I want you here, living at the Bluffs so that I can watch over you and keep you safe. I know that you asked Richard to take you home, but I'm asking you to reconsider. Please. Stay here with me."

A minute ago, fear had coursed through her veins and

apprehension had strangled her. But now his voice reached out to her, his piercing eyes held her captive.

"I'll think about it."

"Good."

She turned and all but ran down the hall, taking the steps two at a time. *Be-witch-ed.*

The word became three syllables and pounded in her head like a rampant mantra as she rounded the turn in the hallway and headed back for the main section of the house. That's how Claire would describe Becca's bizarre attraction to David. As for Becca, she couldn't explain it at all.

Richard was waiting for her at the door to the guest room. "You have visitors."

"Detective Megham."

"No. He called and said he's been detained by a new emergency. It's Claire Cavendish and a young man named Larry Gayle."

"Oh, no, not Claire. Not here. Does Claire seem all right?"

"To the contrary. She seems extremely upset. They declined to come in so I suggested they wait for you under the gazebo in the garden."

"Thanks, Richard."

She stopped in the kitchen for a glass of ice water before heading out to the gazebo. If it had been later than noon, she'd have opted for a stiff drink. Claire visiting the Bluffs when just a glimpse of the place made her tremble in fear. There was no way in the world this was going to be good.

Chapter Eleven

Larry's muscles flexed and released in rapid succession, making his breathing shallow and his chest ache as if someone had pounded a fist into his rib cage. Claire sat a few feet away, perched on the edge of a circular garden bench that had been built into the gazebo.

She was weak and yet determined, whimpering like a sick puppy one minute, insisting they had to save Becca the next. He'd never seen her like this, a cross between the preabduction Claire and the empty husk of humanity she'd sunk into right after the attack.

He felt like a heel for bringing her up here and putting her through this, even though it was her idea. But Becca was so protective of Claire, she might leave David Bryson just to relieve Claire's fears.

Claire turned and looked back toward the Bluffs. "What do you think is taking her so long?"

"Who knows? I can't even imagine what she's doing in there. No woman in their right mind would willingly spend the night with that freaky lunatic."

"Becca doesn't see him that way. He's bewitched her the same way he did Tasha."

"And we know how Tasha ended up."

Bitterness rolled and bucked inside him. He'd been

crazy about Tasha Pierce and finally gotten her to go out with him a time or two. Then the hotshot doctor had moved back to town and bought the Bluffs. And one look from David was all it had taken. Crook his little finger and Tasha had fallen faster and harder than a sky diver with a ripped parachute. Now Becca was making the same stupid mistake, and just when he was hoping they would become more than friends.

He looked up at the sound of crunching leaves. Becca was hurrying across the lawn in their direction, her blond hair catching the wind and dancing in the sunlight. She was staring at him as if she wouldn't mind running an ice pick through his heart. And still she looked beautiful.

Damn David Bryson. But he wouldn't win this time. Larry would see to that.

BECCA WALKED RIGHT PAST Larry and sat down next to Claire. She put an arm around her thin shoulders and hugged her before directing her full attention to Larry. "You shouldn't have brought her here. You know how this place upsets her."

Claire turned to Becca, her eyes glossy, as if someone had sprayed a fine film over them. "He didn't bring me, Becca. I called him. I couldn't leave you up here with that monster."

"Look at me, sweetie. I'm fine. David's not a monster. He's my friend."

"No. He's just pretending to be your friend. Please, Becca, come with us. While you still can."

Claire was trembling, and Becca's heart ached just seeing her in this condition. But Claire was sick. She needed help and understanding, not being dragged around by Larry Gayle on a rescue mission that had no basis. She hugged Claire again and then walked over to

Larry, not stopping until they were practically toe-to-toe. "I'm sorry about your car, Larry, but it wasn't my fault. Someone ran me off the road. Still, I'll pay whatever the insurance doesn't cover."

"If I'd known you were driving up to the freak's castle, I would never have let you borrow the damn car."

"I know. I shouldn't have lied to you. I'm sorry about that, too, but I had to see him."

"So it seems. A nice little tryst with the devil. You must like it since you're still here."

"It's not like that."

"Yeah. Then why don't you tell me what it's like, 'cause that's sure how it looks to me and how it's going to look to everyone else in town."

The insinuation twisted inside her, probably because it wasn't that far from the truth. But whatever she felt for David, it was none of Larry's business. She struggled to keep her tone calm, for Claire's sake. "I want you to take Claire home now, and don't bring her out here again."

A high-pitched wail, sounding more like the squawk of a bird than a young woman, pierced the morning air. "No. No. No."

They both turned to Claire. She was hugging her arms around her chest and rocking back and forth. She stopped when she saw them looking at her and put a hand out toward Becca.

"Please come with us. Please. This place is part of the evil; I can feel it right here." She placed both hands over her chest as if holding her heart in place.

Becca dropped to her knees at Claire's feet and took Claire's trembling hands in hers. "The fear is in your mind. This is just a house, Claire. Nothing more than stones and wood and glass."

"No!" She shook her head almost violently. "It's more than that. Tasha came here and she died here."

"Tasha was killed in an explosion. That had nothing to do with the house or with David."

"Please, just come with us, Becca."

"I can't. Not yet. But don't worry about me. I'll be fine and you will, too. You just need to take your medicine and get some rest." She stood and walked back to Larry, standing close so that she could keep her voice low. "Do you see what you've done? How could you bring her here knowing how upset she's been since the near attack the other night?"

"She wanted to come."

"She's out of her head. Take her home and be gentle with her. Don't say anything else to upset her."

"I'm not the one who's upsetting her. You are. You're upsetting all of us and behaving totally irresponsibly. We're not leaving here without you."

Her anger spun out of control. "I'm perfectly capable of making my own decisions about where I go and whom I go with."

He wrapped his hand around the soft muscles of her upper arm. "I'm driving you home. I'm not losing my woman to some freaking madman again."

His woman? Emotions knotted inside her, then swelled until she thought she might explode. "I was never your woman, Larry. We were friends, and that's all."

"We would have become more if that hideous beast hadn't taken over your mind."

Becca's muscles tensed to the point of aching. Claire, Larry, a killer in a McFarland Leary mask—all slipping over the edge of sanity—or else she was. She tried to pull away from Larry, but his fingers dug into her flesh and he twisted her arm until pain shot up the muscles and into her shoulders. She could scream for help, but that would only upset Claire more.

"Whose car are you in?" she asked, looking around and not seeing a vehicle.

"Mrs. Cavendish's Ford. It's parked in front of the house." He shoved her in that direction, his hand still gripping her arm.

Claire started crying. "Don't hurt Becca, Larry. Don't you turn into a monster, too. I can't take this. I just can't."

"It's okay, sweetie." Becca felt the pressure of the situation squeezing her head like a vice, but she had to at least sound in control for Claire's sake. "I'll ride back to town with you."

"I didn't want him to hurt you," she whispered, her voice ragged. "I don't want anyone to hurt you."

"Stop sniveling," Larry ordered. "Becca said she's coming with us, and that's what you wanted." He finally let go of Becca, though he walked so close that his arm brushed against hers and she could smell the perspiration that beaded on his flesh in spite of the coolness of the day.

This was a side of Larry she'd never seen. It stunned her that she could have thought she knew him well, had considered him a friend without ever dreaming he could be this callous. Yet he'd never made a secret of how he felt about David.

Amazingly Claire pulled herself together enough to stand and start walking toward the car, though she looked as if she might drop into a faint at any second. Detective Megham would be upset when he arrived and Becca wasn't there, but he'd get over it. After all, he was the one who blew off the appointment, and he couldn't expect her to put her life on hold just so she could be harassed by him.

DAVID STOOD IN THE DOORWAY watching Becca deal with her two friends. After what she'd seen in the library, he'd fully expected her to be gone when he left the lab and came to lunch, but here she was, and all he felt was that strange jumping of his heart that he always experienced when she was near.

He wasn't surprised that Larry Gayle had shown up, not as furious as he'd been when David had talked to him on the phone last night. But he was surprised he'd brought Claire Cavendish with him, especially now that he saw her from a few yards away. Her flesh was pale and her gait unsteady, as if just walking to the old Ford parked in his driveway was taking all the strength she could muster.

David pushed out the door unnoticed as Larry and Becca neared the car, Claire still several feet behind them. Evidently Becca was leaving with them, without even a look back at the Bluffs. He'd expected her to leave, and still he dreaded it so much that the metallic taste of desperation filled his mouth and dried his throat.

As they neared the car, he saw Larry grab Becca's arm roughly. The move caught him off guard, but his muscles tensed and he stepped outside, staying half hidden behind a cluster of thick shrubbery.

"I said I would go with you. Now, get your hands off me."

Becca's voice was low, barely carrying to where he was standing, but there was no mistaking the tone.

Larry maintained the grip. "Is that what you say to the freak when he touches you?"

"He's not a freak. He's kind and smart and he's—"

"And he's not too fond of watching someone man-handle a woman."

Larry dropped his hold on Becca and turned to face David, his mouth twisted into a scowl, his chin jutted forward. "I've come to take Becca home, and you need to stay out of this. Moriah's Landing has had enough of you, and so have I."

"I see. Becca, do you want to get in this man's car?"

Becca looked first at Larry and then back to Claire. She dropped back and wrapped a hand around Claire's waist, before finally letting her gaze settle on David. "I don't want to go with him, but I need to take care of Claire. She shouldn't be out here in the condition she's in."

"In that case, I'll have Richard drive you and Claire into town."

Relief eased the lines in Becca's neck and face. "I'd appreciate that, David." She turned to Claire. "David's butler is going to drive you home, Claire. I'll go with you. He's a kind and sensitive man, and he'll take good care of us."

Larry beat a fist into the hood of the Ford, then glared at David, his expression making it clear that he would have liked to plant his fist somewhere else.

David met his glaring stare, amazed at how badly he ached to leave the camouflaging cover of the shrubs and get in the man's face. Only to do that would expose his deformities, put them on display in the bright sunlight. And then he'd have to watch as repulsion drove Becca away forever.

"This is private property, Larry, and your welcome has run out."

"I'm leaving, but this isn't the end of this. Your days in this town are numbered. Count on it." He opened the car door and folded his six-foot-plus frame behind the steering wheel. The elbow of his left arm jutted out the open window as he turned the key in the ignition and gunned the engine before turning back for a parting shot. "You can sleep with the devil, Becca, just don't expect to get your soul back when you're done." A second later his tires squealed as he jerked the car in gear and took off.

David watched the car skid around the first turn, barely missing the ditch that bordered the drive. He had the crazy feeling that his life was like the car, spiraling out of control. And he was pulling Becca along with him, enmeshing her in his life and pulling her into danger that he had no idea how to stop. She was certain the danger was her doing. He knew better. The danger had always lain with him.

"Thanks, David. That was so…"

"Human."

"That's not what I was going to say."

But it was what she meant. He could see it in her eyes. And for the first time in five years he felt almost human again. Too bad that feelings could not be trusted. He should turn and go back inside, leave things as they were, but he couldn't. "Will you be coming back with Richard?"

"I'm not sure."

"Then think about it. You'll be safe here, and…" He wasn't one to beg, yet the need inside him was so strong. "I want you with me, Becca." With that he turned and walked inside, hating himself for needing her when Tasha's memory was so real inside him. When Tasha's murder had not been vindicated.

DETECTIVE MEGHAM STOOD next to the chief of police while a hoard of reporters pushed around them with cameras, microphones and wagging pencils. The chief had called a press conference to detail the newly discovered identity of the body that had been found a few days ago. Sally Evers, twenty-two, a recent graduate of Heathrow College who was interviewing in a neighboring district for a teaching job. She'd apparently rented a car and driven to Moriah's Landing for a few days' vacation before driving back to Missouri.

But, as Megham had suspected, the chief wasn't telling much more. He'd left out the fact that the jugular had been severed with two deep cuts, and he'd neither confirmed or denied the leak that the killer had left initials M.L. carved into the woman's stomach. He'd merely stated the facts concerning the methods used by the killer were confidential so as not to impede the investigation and eventual arrest of the man responsible for the murder.

But Megham wasn't wasting his time searching the cemetery for some damn ghost. As far as he was concerned, David Bryson was the major suspect. He didn't have proof, but in the past his intuition in cases like this had been right a lot more often than it had been wrong.

They'd pretty much pinpointed the time of death, and Bryson had been seen in town that night, as always lurking in the shadows and having little to say to anyone. That gave him the opportunity, and any healthy adult male with access to a sharp blade—as in a scalpel—had the ability.

That left motive. Insanity required no real motive, and everyone knew that the beast on the hill was crazy. He'd been questioned in the murders twenty years ago and he'd been questioned in the explosion that took his fiancée's life five years ago.

Megham had an idea that when the evidence started falling into place, it would be like a row of dominoes dropping, one after another. When the last one fell, Bryson would be behind bars and Moriah's Landing would go back to being the peaceful sort of town Prissy had wanted to retire to.

Now Megham had a new kink in the case. Becca Smith, a seemingly intelligent woman, had apparently become involved with Bryson. While he hated to see Becca put herself into that kind of danger, there wasn't a lot he could do about it, so he might as well use the situation to his advantage. As soon as this press conference was over, he'd go to the Bluffs and interview her. He was already late for their appointment. It would give him the opportunity he needed to get inside that stone wall and look around, get a feel for the place. All he'd need was one good piece of evidence for the court to grant a search warrant.

"Do you foresee an arrest anytime soon?"

"I'll defer the questions about the actual investigation to Detective Megham, as he's heading up the case with the full assets of the department behind him."

Chief Redfern nodded to him to take the question from the saucy female reporter from the local news TV station. He cleared his throat while weighing his words. "We don't foresee an imminent arrest, but we are investigating every lead that comes our way." A dozen reporters started clamoring for his attention. He pointed to a young Asian man in a dark gray suit.

"Do you have any suggestions for how women should protect themselves while this maniac is on the loose?"

"If they go out at night, they should go out in groups or with an escort. Above all, stay out of situations that leave them vulnerable, such as walking home alone at night or being out near the wharf area alone. At this point, we believe that the victim was alone and in an unprotected area at the time of the attack.''

''How did you reach that conclusion?''

''The perpetrator did a good job of avoiding witnesses. Apparently no one saw or heard anything.''

''Is it possible that the villain knew the victim?''

''Anything's possible.''

He fielded a dozen more questions, all more or less versions of the first few before the chief called a halt to the conference. He sucked in a double helping of relief. Talking to reporters was the part of his job he liked the least, but the public had a right to know—just not the right to know enough to interfere with his investigation. These conferences were always stretched along a fine line of fact and omissions.

He stepped away and headed back inside the station house. Once inside, a spurt of adrenaline revived him to the point he couldn't wait to get on his way. Next stop the Bluffs and hopefully a chance to meet Dr. David Bryson in person. Wealthy, renowned scientist gone mad.

THE SUN GLINTED OFF the rocks as David stood on the top of the cliff, scattering the petals of white roses. It wasn't his usual day to honor Tasha's memory in this way, but since Becca had come into his life, the need to remember every detail about Tasha had swelled to a crescendo, blaring inside his brain.

But try as he might to preserve it, the memory of Tasha had started to dim. Worse, it had begun to merge with images of Becca. At times when he looked into Becca's eyes, it seemed to be Tasha staring back at him. It was as if Tasha's spirit haunted the Bluffs, calling to him, whispering his name in the dark of night. But when he closed his eyes, it was Becca's smile he saw.

His mind shuffled back through the years. It had been different with Tasha from the very beginning. She'd triggered something inside him, released the valve that kept the black, angry secrets of his past locked safely away. She was the first person he'd ever told what it was like growing up in a shanty behind the wharf area where men from town knocked on his mother's door day and night. Tasha had neither faulted nor excused his mother's lifestyle, except to say that his mother couldn't have been all bad. She'd given him life, and Tasha loved her for that.

No one gets to choose their family. The best we can do is just love them and take them as they are. That had been Tasha's response not only to his past but to the way her family had rebelled against her dating him.

He had loved her so, been certain that he'd never love anyone else, yet his obsession with Becca grew more intense, more agonizing with every second he spent in her presence. Not only was it spoiling his memory of Tasha, it was interfering with his work—the one thing that had seemed to make any sense at all over the last five years.

He thrived on working alone in his lab, and that was one of the reasons he'd moved from being a practicing physician to a medical scientist. He wanted hypotheses that could be proved true or false if the experiments were thorough and ruled out all variables.

He liked making a difference, not in one life, but in countless thousands. Like now. He was so close to another major breakthrough, this time in an area that could save the lives of people who'd already been given a death sentence, good, hardworking people like Brie's mother. Pamela Dudley's physician had heard of David's research and sent David her medical records.

Pamela had been one of the few ladies in town who hadn't snubbed her nose at David's mother, and that had earned her a place in his heart. He hadn't been able to save his mother from the cancer that had robbed her of the will to keep fighting for life, but he still had a chance to save Mrs. Dudley, to give her the opportunity to see her grandchild grow up.

He dropped the last few roses without bothering to scatter the petals. Work was what he needed now. It was the only way to keep the little sanity he had left.

But even as he made his way back to the lab, thoughts of Tasha and Becca tiptoed through his mind. Tasha was dead, but he owed her justice, had to find the man who'd blown up the boat and stolen her life's breath. Becca was alive, but she'd never be able to love a man whose heart had been broken in so many pieces it would never be whole again. And she'd never desire a body as hideously deformed as the one that encased his soul and mind.

And still he wanted her.

BECCA KEPT UP a steady conversation with Claire on the way back into town. She chattered about the weather, the leaves that had already begun their transformation to the glorious reds and golds that would set the woods on fire in the next few weeks, but her attempts to lighten the mood had little or no effect on Claire or the pit of despair she'd settled into.

"Do you mind if I use your phone?" Becca asked as Richard turned onto Main Street. "I'd like to call Mrs. Cavendish and let her know we're on our way. I'm sure she's worried about Claire."

"Help yourself."

She dialed the number. Mrs. Cavendish answered on the first ring. "Hello."

"It's me, Becca. I'm bringing Claire home."

"Is she all right?"

"She's—very upset, almost catatonic."

"Oh, my poor baby. He hasn't hurt her, has he?"

"No, Larry didn't hurt her, but he should have never taken her up to the Bluffs. I can't imagine what possessed him."

"I didn't mean Larry. I meant that beast. Larry just left. He said Dr. Bryson was holding you and Claire at his castle."

Becca struggled to contain her anger. "Larry lied, Mrs. Cavendish. Dr. Bryson's butler is driving us home because Larry was turning violent. We'll be there in a few minutes."

"Oh, dear. I was so afraid. I was just about to call the police when you called."

"Then I'm glad I caught you first. Claire's okay, but she'll need her medicine and you may want to call her doctor. Most of all, you need to keep her away from Larry Gayle."

"You can count on that. He told me he and Claire were going to lunch when they left here in my car. I would have never let him take her to the Bluffs."

"I know." Becca's heart went out to Mrs. Cavendish as she ended the conversation and broke the connection. The family had been through so much. Claire's abduction, then Mr. Cavendish's untimely death in a construction site accident. Now Becca was pulling them into more trouble.

When Richard turned the corner onto Front Street, she could see Mrs. Cavendish and Tommy, her teenage son, standing on the porch. As soon as he slowed and pulled to the curb, they rushed down the steps to the car.

Becca jumped from the car and went around to help them get Claire from the back seat. Claire wasn't trembling anymore, and some of the color had come back to her face, but her eyes were still wide and glazed over, the pupils enlarged.

Tommy practically lifted his sister out of the car and set her down on the sidewalk. "I'm going to give Larry a piece of my mind. You can believe that," he muttered, supporting most of Claire's body weight.

Mrs. Cavendish's eyes were moist and red, and she brushed the back of her sleeve across them. Becca gave her a comforting hug, then leaned against the back fender of the car and watched the three of them, their arms intertwined, slowly climb the steps. This was the house they'd lived in all of Claire's life. They belonged here. She didn't.

I want you with me, Becca.

David's words floated through her mind, as hypnotic and real as if he were here beside her. "Why do you want me?"

"Excuse me."

"Sorry, Richard. I guess I was talking to myself." He nodded, as if he understood perfectly.

She couldn't stay here and she had nowhere else to go—except to a man who'd invaded her mind, stirred passion that she had no idea she was capable of feeling. A man who lived in an isolated castle high on a cliff.

A man whose heart belonged to a dead woman.

Only a fool would make a choice like that. A fool or else a woman who was totally bewitched—or in love.

Chapter Twelve

Becca moved around the small room, packing the last of her clothes and meager belongings into cardboard boxes that Richard had obtained for her from the neighborhood grocer. At first she'd planned on taking only a few essentials, but when she realized how sparse her entire stash of worldly possessions actually amounted to, she decided to pack everything. A woman without a past traveled light.

She'd drop off a few boxes of books, photographs, summer clothes and souvenirs at Threads and take the rest of her belongings with her to the Bluffs. There was certainly plenty of room there. The issue was that if and when she decided to move out of the Bluffs, she didn't want it to be a major undertaking. Easy come, easy go. That was the only way this could work.

Richard had offered to help with the packing, as had Mrs. Cavendish, but Becca was more comfortable sifting through her own things and saying goodbye to the room and another time in her life that would never return. A rented room wouldn't mean much to most people, but it was as much home as any Becca could remember.

Although the tiny room didn't compare to the grandeur of the Bluffs, it had been hers. The Bluffs belonged to David and to Tasha's memory, perhaps even to Tasha's ghost. Certainly the spirit of David's dead fiancée seemed to inhabit the place. Apprehension gathered inside her in prickly sensations and jabbing bouts of nausea. There was a good chance she was about to make the biggest mistake of her life.

Had Tasha Pierce wondered that same thing when she'd gone to the Bluffs on the last night of her life? Was that why her spirit still roamed the halls and perhaps left cold spots in the house where she'd been supposed to live as Mrs. David Bryson?

She pushed the ridiculous ideas from her mind. It was the attempt on her life and Claire's emotional state that was spooking her so. The Bluffs was just a house. David Bryson was just a man.

And if she was wrong about that, heaven help her.

"DID YOU CALL DAVID and tell him I was coming home with you?" she asked as Richard pulled away from the Cavendish home, the back seat and the trunk of the car loaded to capacity.

"I did. He seemed pleased, and he said to tell you that you have a visitor on the way."

"Detective Megham must be determined to see me in spite of our missed appointments."

"Apparently. The detective says he has important news."

News—or a warrant for David's arrest. The apprehension that had been churning inside her settled into full-blown dread as they started toward Threads to drop off a few boxes before heading up Old Mountain Road.

MEGHAM PERCHED ON THE EDGE of the antique Victorian chair in the drawing room, awkwardly, as if he thought the furniture might not support his weight. Becca sat on the sofa, facing him. He'd wanted David to be present for the questioning, but David had refused, saying he was involved in an experiment that he couldn't leave at the time. The best he could offer was to take part in the discussion via speakerphone.

That bit of news hadn't surprised Becca. She'd never seen David outside the dark and shadows, and she hadn't expected he'd just walk into the drawing room as if it was an everyday matter. Megham, however, was obviously irritated that David had refused to show up in person. He finished questioning Becca first, then had Richard get his boss on the phone. His questions to him were pointed and curt.

"I realize murder is not high on your priority list, Dr. Bryson, but I'd like to hear your version of what happened on Old Mountain Road yesterday."

David wasted no words in describing how he'd heard the crash, then found Becca slumped over the wheel of the wrecked car.

"So you never saw the driver of the other vehicle?" Megham asked, his tone suggesting he didn't totally believe David.

"That's what I said."

"Well, at least you were out of the house. From what I hear, you don't venture out during the daylight hours."

"Is my lifestyle part of this investigation?"

"It could be, before it's all said and done. Why did you bring Becca Smith back to your house instead of taking her home or to the hospital?"

"Is it a crime to take care of a friend after she's had a bad experience?"

"I'll ask the questions here, Bryson. You just answer,'' Megham sputtered, becoming more flustered by the second. ''Why did you bring Becca to the Bluffs?''

''I can answer that,'' she said.

Megham stared at her coldly. ''Okay. Let's hear it.''

''David and I are friends. I was frightened and upset, and he took care of me.''

Megham leaned forward, his bushy brows knitted and drawn tight over his eyes. ''You have strange taste in friends.''

''Nonetheless I came here by choice.''

He shook his head, glaring at her as if he thought she'd taken complete leave of her senses.

''So what is this news you mentioned when you called earlier?'' Becca asked.

Megham pulled a wrapped cigar out of his shirt pocket, worried it for a few seconds, then stuck it back in his pocket. ''We've located the car used to force you off the road, or at least what's left of it.''

''Where?'' she asked, springing to full attention.

''On the outskirts of town.''

She sucked in a grateful breath. ''Surely if you found the car, you can track it down to its owner.''

''We did. The car was stolen from the driveway of a retired couple down on Armstrong Street. They're visiting their daughter in Illinois, didn't even know it was missing until we got the phone number from a neighbor and called them.''

''But the car should have fingerprints.''

''If the guy left prints, they're destroyed now. He set the vehicle on fire. The only reason we were able to match it to the owner was that the car exploded and sent the license plate careering through space like a missle. It landed a few yards away, basically undamaged.''

Her surge of optimism disappeared as quickly as it had bloomed. "So that leaves us nowhere again."

"Pretty much." He finally scooted back in his chair and crossed an ankle over his knee. "You know, Becca, you've pretty much set yourself up as a target."

"How is that?" David asked, his voice booming from the speakerphone.

"Hanging out with you. You're not the most popular man in town, you know?"

"Who Becca chooses as a friend doesn't give anyone the right to claim open season on her."

"I'm not saying it does," Megham answered. "I just think she'd be wise to stay away from you."

"I'm not just 'hanging out' with David, Detective, I'm living at the Bluffs for a while."

His face hardened into a misshapen sculpture. "Then I'd say you're making a very big mistake. There's already been one woman murdered in this town. I'd hate to see you become the second."

"If idle insinuations are all you have to offer, Megham, I think I'll get back to work. I'm sure Becca has better things to do with her time, too. I'll have my butler show you to the door."

Megham's face turned a blustery red, but he had no comeback for David. Funny, but in this situation, it was David who seemed the older and wiser of the two men, certainly the one in control. And she felt incredibly young and vulnerable, unsure of herself in every way. But she'd have to grow up fast. Her life might very well depend on it. And the last thing she wanted to become was a pawn in a game orchestrated by a murderer.

ON WEDNESDAY AFTERNOON, two days after Becca had moved in with David Bryson, Brie Pierce sat in the wooden swing on the Cavendish front porch, using her right foot to maintain the steady, hypnotizing motion of the swing. The chains squeaked slightly, and condensation from the glass of lemonade she was holding rolled across her fingers. Claire sat in the birchwood rocker, rocking back and forth and toying with a shredded tissue.

Claire had called and asked her to come by for a few minutes, said she needed to talk to her, but so far Claire had said very little. Still, Brie sensed something different about her, a slight change in the agitation Claire had begun demonstrating after the abduction five years ago.

Brie sipped the lemonade. "Are you still worried about Becca?"

"Not as much as I was, but I'd feel better if she wasn't staying with David Bryson."

"My family says the same thing. Have you heard from her since she moved out?"

"She called this morning."

"How did she sound?"

"The same as always, but I know she's falling under David's spell, the same way Tasha did. Sometimes I think he's McFarland Leary reincarnated."

"I don't even want to think about that." Brie watched a squirrel scurry around the roots of an oak tree, then scamper off across the yard. "You said when you called that you needed to talk."

Claire chewed on the end of a fingernail, then clasped her hands together in her lap. "I think my memory of the abduction is starting to come back. I'm remembering things that had been lost before, sights and even smells. I remember the same things I've always remembered, but everything's more intense and I seem to move further into the setting, as if I'm there again."

The words came out in a rush, the syllables running over one another so badly that it took Brie a minute for the message to sink in. When it did, she shuddered and a lump settled in her stomach like a ball of cold wax. "Do you remember a face?"

"No, not yet. But last night I was in my room alone, staring out the window, and I saw myself lying on a gurney in a dark room. I had tubes attached to my arms and one stuck down my throat. I was trying to pull away, but I was so weak I couldn't move. I opened my mouth to scream and something hot and sticky, like blood, gurgled from my throat and ran down my neck."

Brie stopped the swing, reached across the space that separated them and took Claire's hands in hers. "How horrible. Let's not even talk about it."

"But I have to remember. I *want* to remember. It's the only way I'll ever be able to get past the terror and have any kind of normal life."

"I guess. I keep thinking about the man who did that to you. I wonder if he's the man who killed Sally Evers."

"I wonder the same thing, and sometimes I think I would have been better off if he'd killed me, too."

"Don't talk that way. It's always better to be alive. You'll get better. I know you will."

"I keep hoping."

"You will. I'm just so thankful Geoffrey happened by when he did the other night when you and Becca were almost attacked."

"He called me yesterday."

"Really? What did he want?"

"He just asked how I was doing. I don't know him that well, but he seems such a nice person."

"I don't know, Claire. Drew doesn't fully trust him,

not since Dr. Leland Manning was arrested, but then Drew can be a tad suspicious.''

"That's a politician for you."

"True, but Geoffrey does seem upset about something, or else he and Drew's dad have had a falling out we don't know about. He's moved down to the family beach house, doesn't even attend family dinners and celebrations anymore.''

"At any rate, he saved my life, and I was glad for the chance to thank him. I was too upset to have anything to do with him that night.''

"Just don't trust him too much. That's all I'm saying. Now, about these memories—have you talked to your doctor about them?''

"Yes, and he agrees that I might be on the brink of remembering vital information.'' Claire let go of Brie's hands and started rocking again, slower this time, as if each movement took effort. "I'm thinking I should go back to the cemetery, that if I stand next to the mausoleum where I was abducted I might finally remember the face of the man who abducted me.''

"It's too risky. Your emotional state is too fragile. Just give yourself time. You'll remember when your mind and body are ready.''

"I suppose. It's just that I'm so worried about Becca.''

"I know. We all are, but Becca's a very capable woman. I'm sure she didn't just move into the Bluffs without giving it serious thought.'' Brie stood and gave Claire a hug. She couldn't stay much longer. Drew was speaking to the local teachers association tonight, and he wanted her to go with him. And she loved being at his side. She loved him so.

She wished for that same kind of love for Becca and

for Claire one day. But mostly, she just prayed they stayed safe and sane.

BECCA RAN HER fingers along the worn drapes in the drawing room, envisioning the way the room would look when she had the new ones ready to hang. She wished she had more time to devote to the redecorating, but with dresses to finish for the Fall Extravaganza, a couple of weeks absence from Threads was all she could spare right now—time to recover completely from the wreck. Time to adjust to living with David.

Her contact with David had been minimal since moving in. He was in his lab from daybreak until dark, and the few times she'd seen him at all had been from a distance, down the length of one of the dark hallways. Yet she sensed his presence everywhere, his and Tasha's. And he'd visited her in her dreams every night, each one becoming more and more erotic, as if her unconscious were compensating for his physical slights.

In spite of David's absence, Richard and the entire staff went out of their way to make her feel welcome, but she knew that the changes around the rambling castle made them all a little nervous. Security was tighter, with newer and even more technically sophisticated equipment mounted at the electric gates and around the property. And the doors to the main house were kept locked, even during the day.

Her arrival had changed the beautiful castle to a guarded fortress, all David's way of protecting her, though he never mentioned it.

She wandered the hallway, back up the stairs and to the spot where she had felt the rush of cold air before. The hairs on her neck stood on end as a sheet of icy air climbed her spine and seemed to settle deep in her bones. But the house was old. Surely there was a rational explanation for the change in temperature.

She tried the door. It was locked tight, just as it had been before, though she hadn't encountered any other doors inside the house that were locked.

The cleaning woman was in a room a few doors down the hall. She could hear her walking around, humming a tune as she worked. Her keys were still in the door, dangling from the lock, inviting, beckoning.

Becca looked away, then back again. No one would miss the keys in the seconds it would take her to unlock the other door. As if in a trance, she walked to the open door, slipped her fingers over the keys and silently pulled them from the lock. Hands shaking, she tried several keys in the new lock, finally finding one that turned easily. Then, barely daring to breathe, she turned the knob, pushed the door open and stepped inside the room.

Stepped inside a shrine to Tasha Pierce.

She shivered as her gaze swept the room. It was just as it must have looked five years ago. Bouquets of fresh white roses filled cut-crystal vases. Two champagne flutes set on a silver tray, ready for toasting. And the bridal dress, a frothy concoction of silk and lace, lay across the bed, the train flowing to the floor, the headpiece and veil like a crown above it all.

Everything ready for the bride who had never made it to her wedding.

Becca staggered backward, consumed by an emptiness that left her weak. So much love. So needlessly lost. David and Tasha, soul mates who'd been torn apart by an explosion that had never been explained.

Her mind seemed to travel back in time and link with Tasha's. Blinking back tears, Becca crossed the room and picked up the exquisite headpiece and veil. She slipped it on, adjusting the veil so that it fell over her face. Then, carefully, as if the fabric might dissolve at her touch, she lifted the wedding dress and held it to her shoulders.

Her reflection stared back at her from the angled floor mirror and she could feel the swish of silk around her legs and ankles. Closing her eyes tight against the light and the glare of reality, she swayed back and forth, envisioned herself dancing with David. The moment was incredibly sweet.

She imagined David's lips on hers, his hands tangled in her hair, pulling her close. "I love you," she whispered, not even aware of what she was saying. Only aware of the intensity of the passion that swirled inside her.

"Tasha!"

She opened her eyes with a start and stared at the man who stood in front of her, seeing him for the first time in the bright light of day. It was a sight she would never forget.

Chapter Thirteen

The wedding dress slipped from Becca's shaking fingers and pooled at her feet. David's eyes were dark, penetrating, his gaze so intense, she felt as if he held her with some invisible force. She was conscious of the thick locks of dark hair that fell across his brow, of the scar that ran down the side of his face, of the jut of his strong jaw, but they were drowned in the emotions that swelled and churned inside her.

"You had no business coming into this room, Becca." His voice was bitter, accusing.

"I'm sorry, David. I'm really sorry." She took a step toward him, but he turned away and faced the wall.

"Just get out of here. That's all I ask. Leave me some small shred of pride."

Bending, she picked up the dress and spread it across the bed just as she'd found it.

"Are you happy now, Becca? You wanted to see the hideous wound and now you have. It'll make a great horror story to tell your friends on dark, stormy nights."

"The scar's not so bad, David."

"It made you sick to look at it. Do you think I'm blind, that I didn't see the repulsion that turned your stomach? You couldn't even look at me."

"It was just the initial shock. It's not important. It's not who you are."

"It's *all* I am. All that's left of me. Now, please leave this room, Becca. You have free run of the rest of the house and I'll make certain you never have to face me again."

"Would you like me to leave the Bluffs?"

"No. Please, don't go. You'll be safe here."

Safe but alone. She ached to go to him and wrap her arms around him. But he stood with his back to her, his stature ramrod straight.

"Don't climb back into your shell, David. Please. Don't leave me."

"I'm not going anywhere."

But he was. He was going back to some dark place inside himself where she'd never be able to find him. A place where only memories of Tasha lived and a time when he'd been whole and free. Back to a life that had no room for her or any of the outside world.

He had never been hers, and yet her heart seemed to be drying up inside her as she left the room and walked away. Even from a watery grave, Tasha had won.

DAVID STOOD IN THE HALLWAY watching Becca, his insides a massive bundle of raw nerves and ragged pain. When he'd stepped inside the door and seen Becca standing there, he'd almost lost his grip on reality. For a second his mind had seen Tasha, and the past had come down and buried him under a rush of cruel memories.

When the moment had passed, he'd lashed out at Becca, the last person he'd ever wanted to hurt. But at best he was only a mangled, twisted shell of a man. Now Becca had seen that for herself. He'd witnessed the shock in her eyes and then he'd watched them change to pity. It was almost more than he could bear.

He should have never given into the desires that had driven him, never sought her out in the dark of night. His obsession for her had been unquenchable. It still was.

Even now, he ached to go to her and take her in his arms. Longed to make love with her as if it was the last night of the world. But she'd never want him the way he wanted her.

He swallowed his painful need for her, knew he'd go to the secret bookcase opening that led to the cavernous catacombs hidden below the house in the bowels of the earth. He'd failed everyone in his life who'd ever mattered, and the dank, musky chamber below the earth was the only place that truly welcomed him now.

But at least Becca was safe. He could do that much for her if he couldn't do anything else. He closed the door to "Tasha's" room and turned the key in the lock without looking back. Tasha wasn't in there. She was dead. More than ever, he rued the day he hadn't died with her.

THE NEXT TWO DAYS PASSED in a miserable silence. There was no news from Megham about the man who had run Becca from the road or tried to attack her and Claire, and there had been no arrest in the death of Sally Evers. Worse, Becca hadn't even seen David, though she'd heard him talking to Richard and knew he still went to town every night.

Becca had worked on the plans for redecorating the Bluffs, but her heart was no longer in the project. She just wanted to see David, all of him, scar included. She missed him so.

Feeling too restless to do any kind of meaningful work, she walked to the back door just off the kitchen. Taking the key ring Richard had given her from her pocket, she fit a small bronze key into the lock, turned it, then stepped outside, careful to relock the door behind her. Fluffy white clouds floated overhead, but the sun was hot and had already burned away the early morning fog. Walking gingerly, she made her way down the brick path to the edge of the cliff where she had seen David scattering white roses a few days earlier.

Standing at the top of the cliff, she studied the waters below. Along most of the area's shoreline, a pounding surf splashed over dangerous rocks, but in this spot the cove was protected, almost serene. The perfect spot to moor a small yacht. The spot where the fatal explosion had occurred.

She rubbed her eyes as strange images assaulted her mind. Fire and smoke. The sound of splintering wood and boards crashing into the sea. The smell of burning flesh and gasoline. She rocked backward, almost losing her balance, then reached out and grabbed the sharp edge of a huge boulder to steady herself.

No wonder David could never forget the night Tasha was killed. Becca hadn't even been there and yet she felt the terror churning inside her just thinking about what it must have been like. Was this what Tasha's family felt when they thought about that night? If so, it was easy to understand why Tasha's parents and the rest of the Pierces couldn't let go of the loss enough to forgive David.

She turned at the sound of neighing and spotted David sitting on the back of his horse a few yards away. He looked different. His shaggy hair had been cut and he was clean shaven though he wore a cloak with a hood that covered most of his scar. Still, he took her breath away, and she stood for long moments just staring at him before she noticed another horse, saddled and waiting behind him.

"It's a perfect morning for a ride," he said. "Besides, I thought you might be getting cabin fever. I had the stable hand saddle Stardust for you. She's gentle but spirited. I think you'll like her."

"I'm sure I will." She walked over to the filly, crooning as she did and moving slowly so as not to frighten the majestic animal. "Does this mean you've forgiven me?"

"It means I've missed you."

His voice was husky, low, seductive, and warmth seeped inside her and tugged at her heart. She ached to have him climb down from his horse, take her in his arms and smother her with kisses the way he had the other night.

"I've missed you, too." She took Stardust's reins and hoisted her foot into the saddle. "I'm ready for anything, Dr. Bryson."

THE DAY WAS GOLDEN, brilliant sunshine, leaves tinged with every shade of red imaginable, and as far as David was concerned, all of it paled when compared to the splendor of the woman riding a few feet in front of him. Her long silky hair was pulled up in a knot, and loose tendrils cascaded down and wound into tight curls that bounced along the regal lines of her neck.

It had been pure hell staying away from her the last few days. For five years he'd managed just fine without a woman, but now his body seemed to have adopted a mind of its own. No matter how often he told himself that he had no business even thinking of making love to her, he thought of almost nothing else. He thought of his lips on hers, his hands roaming the soft curves of her neck, fitting over the soft mounds of her breasts, touching and teasing and making her ache for him the way he ached for her.

But there was no way to think of making love to her without remembering how she'd reacted to the sight of his scar. And that was not the worst of what he had to offer.

She reined in Stardust and waited for him to catch up to her. "This is such a beautiful spot. Can we dismount and talk for a while?"

Talk. He'd heard somewhere that the four scariest words a man could hear from a woman were "we need to talk." He'd never realized before now how true that was. "I'm not much of a talker," he said, climbing out of the saddle.

"I've noticed."

He helped her dismount, then tied the two horses to a low-hanging branch. She walked ahead of him, stopping at a flat area covered with a thick carpet of dried leaves.

"It seems so peaceful out here, as if we're a million miles away from all the trouble that's plagued me and Moriah's Landing," she said, dropping to a sitting position.

"What shall we talk about?"

"You."

"Bad boy from the wrong side of the wharf transformed to doctor scientist and then to the beast on the hill. You already know all of that. What else is there to tell?"

"I'd like to know how you can kiss me senseless one minute and pull away the next, why you seek me out to take me horseback riding after going to such lengths to avoid me for the last two days. Is it that you're embarrassed by your scar, because you're afraid of getting involved, or just that you're still in love with Tasha?''

''It's just that I recognize my own weaknesses and I accept the truth. Remember that I'm much older than you.''

''If you accept the truth, why are still hiding behind that hood and cloak?''

''You just don't give up, do you?''

''I can't, David.'' She reached up, took his hand and tugged him down beside her. ''I probably shouldn't care for you, but I do. I care a lot, but before I get in any deeper I need to know if there's a chance for us.''

He took a deep breath, deluged by feelings and needs he didn't understand. But Becca was right. It was time for the truth, for both their sakes. He squeezed her hand, then dropped it as his mind slid into the past. ''I don't know where to start.''

''Just start where it feels right.''

''Then I'll have to start with Tasha.''

Becca felt a sinking sensation, a heavy weight in the pit of her stomach. It seemed ludicrous to be jealous of a dead woman, yet she knew that she was. Jealous, but mostly just unsure whether or not David would ever allow himself to love her or anyone else, or if he planned to live on Tasha's memory for the rest of his life.

Leaves crunched beneath his feet as the heels of his black boots dug into the soft earth. ''Are you sure you want to hear this?''

''I *need* to hear it.''

He hesitated, his lips pressed together, then finally took a deep breath as if he were about to dive into the sea. ''I met Tasha in town a few months after I bought the Bluffs. I knew I was too old for her, but I couldn't deny the attraction or turn down her invitation to go sailing with her and some of her friends. From that moment on, I was hooked. I know falling in love so fast sounds crazy, but that's how it happened.''

"It doesn't sound crazy to me." But it would have before she met David. It was all in a person's frame of reference. "I take it her parents disapproved of your dating."

"To put it mildly. Her family already hated me, insisted I had bought the Bluffs right out from under them while they were waiting for it to go to auction for back taxes. Apparently the deed was in Geoffrey Pierce's name and he mortgaged it to the hilt when he ran up some gambling debts. The family was sure no one else in town could afford it, and intended to buy it back and keep it in the family.''

"Did you know the family planned to buy it back?"

"No. All I knew was that it was up for sale at a good price. It needed some work, and it was much larger and far more lavish than I was looking for, but like everyone else who grew up in Moriah's Landing, I was always awed by the place. And it was the only place available that was large enough to house a full working lab.''

"So even then you planned to work as well as live here?''

"Absolutely. I was going to use the money I'd made through my breakthroughs in genetic research to bring in promising young research scientists and provide them with room, board and enough grant money to live on. I envisioned this place as a mecca for genetic studies that would hopefully lead to major developments in the prevention and cures of terminal illnesses.''

"It could still be that.''

"Maybe one day." But his tone and the shrug of his shoulders indicated he doubted that would ever happen.

"How did Tasha feel about all of that?" she asked.

"She was as excited as I was, thought it was time Moriah's Landing was known for something besides witches and unsolved murders."

"Were you involved with the town's secret medical society?"

His eyes narrowed. "What do you know about that?"

"Nothing, really. I've just heard about it."

"From whom?"

"I don't remember. Kat and Elizabeth were talking about it one night. I think some of the Pierces are members, but I've never been sure if it's actually a medical society or merely a social club."

"It's neither, but to answer your question, I checked it out when I first came back to Moriah's Landing, was in it just long enough to realize that I wanted no part of it."

"Because it involved some of the Pierces?"

"Because it involved unethical research projects—and worse. I'm just beginning to discover how much worse."

His eyes grew darker, shadowed, and Becca felt as if he were changing before her eyes, revisiting his own demons and transforming into the beast everyone took him for. Pinpricks of cold needled her skin, like a spray of finely crushed ice.

"But in spite of all of that, you and Tasha planned to marry and live here in the Bluffs, practically neighbors with the rest of the Pierces."

"She gave her family an ultimatum. Either accept me or lose her. They chose her, at least her parents did. They loved her very much, and she loved them. They wanted to throw an elaborate wedding at the Pierce compound,

but Tasha insisted on a garden wedding at the Bluffs—
the wedding that never happened.''

He stared into space, and Becca felt his pain as if it
had somehow been transferred to her by osmosis. Tears
pooled in her eyes and she brushed at them with the
back of her hand. One minute, he'd been on top of the
world. The next he'd fallen into a black abyss that must
have seemed bottomless.

''It was Tasha's face that kept me going during those
first nights after the explosion when the pain was so
excruciating I wanted to die. And then, when the doctors
finally decided I was well enough to know the truth, they
told me that Tasha had died that night in the explosion.
Her body was never found, only ripped fragments of her
clothing that had washed up on the beach, some pieces
far down the coast.''

Becca searched inside herself, trying to think of something to say, but the only phrases she could think of
sounded trite. So she reached out to him with touch. She
took one of his hands and held it between hers, though
he didn't seem to notice.

''I begged the doctors to let me die, too. If I'd had
the strength, I would have taken my own life. Instead I
dissolved into the pain. Then, when I finally saw myself
in the mirror, I realized Tasha was the lucky one. She
would never have to see the deformed freak I had become. The flesh was literally burned from the right side
of my face and parts of my stomach. I've had countless
skin grafts, so many operations I've long since quit
counting them.''

She lay her head on his shoulder, her heart aching for
him. No wonder he'd locked himself away for years and
come out only at night. ''You're not a freak, David, nor
a beast.''

"How can you say that now that you've seen me?"

"Because I mean it. There's so much more to you, I could forget the scar is even there."

"Could you?"

"Yes. But that still leaves one big unanswered question. Are you still in love with Tasha?"

"I haven't forgotten her."

"No, I'm sure you never will, but that's not what I asked."

He let go of her hand and seemed to draw back into himself. "I know she's dead and that she won't be coming back. But I can't let go of that night, not until I find the man responsible for the explosion. He has to be punished. I owe Tasha that."

"But the police investigation concluded that the explosion was an accident."

"That was only after they couldn't find a way to pin it on me. No evidence of a bomb was ever found, but that doesn't mean there wasn't one. I'm convinced the explosion was deliberate."

"What makes you so sure?"

"I kept the boat in perfect condition and I had checked everything for the honeymoon trip. If there had been any kind of malfunction or leak, I would have caught it. As far as I'm concerned, the only rational explanation is that someone planted explosives on the boat."

"But why would someone do such a horrible thing to Tasha or to you?"

"Tasha was never meant to die. She wasn't even supposed to be at the house that night, much less at the boat. The wedding was scheduled for ten the next morning. We'd had an afternoon prewedding party at her parents' house, and the plans were for her to spend the evening with her parents and attendants and then go to bed early. I was going to stock the boat for our honeymoon trip.''

''What changed her plans?''

''She was young and impetuous. She showed up at the boat, said she had to have some time alone with me. We started kissing and couldn't stop.''

Becca understood that sensation all too well. Even now, in spite of everything, she wanted David, wanted him the same way Tasha must have wanted him that night. The last night of her life.

''We made love that night for the very first time, the only time. Then, when I was telling her goodbye, the boat exploded in a storm of fire and wood and metal, all raining down on us at once. That's the last thing I remember.'' His voice grew husky, and he exhaled sharply.

But she couldn't let this go—not yet. ''And you think that explosion was planned and executed by someone who knew you'd be on the boat?''

''It makes sense, though I haven't been able to find one lead in the case. That's what's driving me positively mad. The answers have to be right here, yet I've looked for five years and can find nothing. I dragged her into the danger, and I let her die.''

''Tasha's death wasn't your fault, David. You can't go on blaming yourself forever.''

''I may not have caused her death, but I didn't stop it.''

His breathing grew ragged, and his voice cracked. The hopeless frustration and desperation were driving him positively mad. But it wasn't his fault. None of it had ever been his fault, no more than what had happened to her had been her fault.

"Please, David, take off the hood. Give me a chance to love the man you are."

He winced, then removed it from his head and let it fall against his cape. The scar was brutal, the flesh pink and puckered, but none of it mattered.

She wrapped her arms around him and held him close, knowing that no matter what she'd said about not letting herself care too much, she already did. Like Tasha, it was as if she was meant to love him.

They held each other for long precious moments. She stroked the back of his head, his shoulders, the corded muscles in his back. The wind whispered against her cheeks. A bird sang. A brown leaf floated down and landed on her leg.

And then David's lips were on hers, and the world ceased to exist. She floated in a sea of desire, aware of nothing except the emotions that swirled inside her. Their breaths mingled, their bodies pressed against each other, and nothing that she could remember had ever felt so right. When he finally pulled away, they were both struggling for breath and for at least a slim hold on reality.

"Whatever you do, David, don't apologize for kissing me, not this time."

"I wasn't going to." His fingers trailed a line down her cheekbone and then pressed against her kiss-swollen lips. "I do think we should get back to the house, though, before I start kissing you again and can't stop with just kisses."

"Would that be so bad?"

"Not for me. I'm just not sure it would be right for you, not yet."

He held her close, and she felt him shudder. She didn't know the full truth about him yet. She was certain of it, but she was just as certain that she'd fallen in love with him. Whatever demons he faced, she could face them with him, as long as she felt his love the way she did at this minute, as long as he didn't pull away and withdraw from her life.

Arm in arm, they walked back to the horses. The words "I love you" hummed inside her, but she didn't say them aloud. She'd save them until she knew the time was right. Hopefully, that would be soon.

THEY TOOK THE LONG WAY back to the Bluffs, riding the crest of the cliff for a while. Azure waters stretched as far as she could see to the east. To the west, the landscape jutted and dipped into rolling grassy hills bordered by woodlands. The air was brisk and invigorating, alive with the smells and sounds of autumn in New England. It was amazing that a day that had started out so badly had turned glorious—all because she was with David. And because they'd talked and kissed and, for the very first time, he'd really opened up to her about his past, shared his hurt, let her see not only the wound and scar that defined the body, but the man inside the body. She still had no guarantee that he felt the same way she did or that he'd ever be ready to move on with his life, but at least she understood him better, and she had to believe there was a chance the two of them could make it as a couple.

Becca Smith. No one from no where, a part of a couple. That in itself was a miracle.

"Hold up a minute," David said, pulling his horse to a dead stop. He'd been riding a few feet in front of her, leading the way, but now his attention was focused on something on the ground. Her gaze followed his to a trail of red. Blood? Maybe.

"What is it?" she asked as the mood shifted from near euphoria to one of dread.

"It's probably just a wounded animal, but I want to check it out."

"Wounded animals can be dangerous."

"I'll be careful. Wait here." He dismounted and secured his horse, then pulled a gun from a leather saddlebag.

"When did you start carrying a gun?"

"At the same time I increased the security for my estate." He disappeared into an area of heavy brush.

She waited for a moment, but as the seconds ticked by with no call from David, the dread became tangible, a nagging uneasiness that riddled her resolve. *The body of a young woman—off Old Mountain Road, close to David Bryson's property.* Only this wasn't *near* David's property. It was *on* his land. Behind a tall stone fence with an electric gate and surveillance cameras. Whatever David had found, it couldn't possibly be another body.

Yet her heart pounded against the walls of her chest as she slid from the saddle and tied Stardust to the branch of a maple tree before setting off to follow him into the woods. When he heard her coming, he took a step backward, his arms outstretched to halt her progress.

"You don't want to see this, Becca."

Chapter Fourteen

David's warning came too late. Becca had already seen the body, stretched out on the grass, the woman's arms and legs twisted at a bizarre angle, a silver-handled knife protruding from her chest. She fell against a tree trunk and grabbed her stomach. She knew she was going to be sick, but there was not one thing she could do about it.

David pulled a clean white handkerchief from his back pocket and handed it to her. She wiped her face, then forced herself to take another look at the body, as shock and nausea gave way to a sick realization. "I know her—*knew* her."

"Who is it?"

"I don't know her name, but I've seen her before. In Wheels, I think."

"Victim number two. Looks like our guy is a serial killer."

"Just like twenty years ago." She walked over to stand by David, still shaking inside, but regaining a bit of her equilibrium. "But how could he get the body in here? He'd have had to hoist it over the fence and drag it all the way back here. There's no way he could have gotten a vehicle through the gate."

"My guess is she came willingly."

"I don't follow."

"People scale the fence all the time, sneak in to get a look at the beast in his lair. I've had kids actually camp out here, a kind of coming-of-age ritual, or an initiation."

"You mean the way Claire had to go inside the mausoleum?"

"Something like that."

"Then you think someone lured the woman here and then killed her?"

"It would have been the easiest way, since we know they didn't come through the gate."

"What kind of monster would do that?"

"The same kind who killed Sally Evers. Don't touch anything. From the looks of the coloring and the texture of the skin, I'd say this body is still warm. We don't want to do anything to contaminate the crime scene. The prints should be fresh enough to lift."

"Unless he wore gloves."

"Even then there could be some way to identify the killer. DNA can be taken from something as seemingly insignificant as one of the killer's hairs."

"You do know that Detective Megham's first suspect will be you."

"As always. For twenty years I've been the scapegoat for everything bad that's ever happened in Moriah's Landing. I'm surprised they didn't try to blame my own mother's death on me."

"Was she murdered?"

"No. She died of an overdose of pain pills when I was seventeen. She had a form of cancer that was incurable, and I don't think she could take living anymore when all she had to look forward to was pain and death.

But I think it's the only thing that happened back then I didn't get blamed for.''

Becca started to walk away but couldn't keep herself from stealing one last look at the body. ''There's something carved on her stomach. Initials.''

He stooped for a better look. ''M.L.''

''McFarland Leary.'' Something snapped inside her and a shudder ripped though her. ''The killer really is the same man who ran me off the road the other day, David. He has to be. Why else would the driver have been wearing that hideous Leary mask?''

''This is all speculation, Becca. Let's just go back to the house and call Megham. This is better left in the hands of the police.''

She was shaking as he led her away, her heart breaking for the young woman whose body lay a few feet away. As few as a couple of hours ago, she could have been alive, laughing and scaling the wall with some man she trusted, maybe was even attracted to. A man with no conscience, who could kill over and over again and never look back.

What kind of man would commit such acts? And how in the world were they going to stop him before she became his victim? He'd already picked her out. Had followed her and Claire home from the restaurant the other night, run her off the road on Sunday. It was the same man. She was sure of it. She didn't know how she knew with such certainty, but she did.

THE INTERVIEW WITH Detective Megham went pretty much as David had anticipated. The man had already made up his mind, and now that he had a bit of evidence to go with his faulty conclusions, he would go after an arrest warrant. Number one—the person who stumbles across a body is always a prime suspect. Two, the body was found on his property. And lastly, he had no alibi for the morning up until the time he took Becca horseback riding.

David wasn't worried about the arrest warrant. They could haul him in and question him all they wanted. When his twenty-four hours were up, they wouldn't have the evidence to justify holding him any longer—unless they manufactured some. That was always a possibility, but he didn't see Megham as the kind of guy who'd go that far.

But the biggest problem was that while Megham worked at putting him away, the real killer was out there, no doubt planning his next attack. And that could very well be against Becca.

"That man is really beginning to irritate me," Becca said the minute the door closed behind Megham.

"I think that's his plan," David said.

"He's so set on arresting you that he didn't even comment on your suggestion that the woman might have come here willingly with the killer."

"He's probably already figured that out, as well."

"I know the killer is the same man who tried to attack Claire and me the other night and then ran me off the road. The mask, the initials. It all adds up."

"But if it's the same man, then he's using a completely different style with you, and that's very unusual for a serial killer. It's as if he's singled you out, has taken more risks to get to you."

David pulled a black notebook from his pocket and started making notes, talking out loud while he wrote. "A man who doesn't buy into the town's hype of a ghost who rose from the dead to kill young maidens, but is crazy enough to play along with the idea."

"Or else it really is McFarland Leary."

"You surely don't believe in ghosts."

"I didn't." Now she wasn't sure. Half the time she felt as if Tasha's ghost still roamed the halls of the Bluffs, that Tasha had entered her mind, haunted her so that she felt Tasha's emotions instead of her own, the way she had when looking over the water where Tasha had been killed. The way she had when she'd held Tasha's wedding dress to her shoulders. And if Tasha's ghost was still present, then McFarland Leary's could be as well.

"The ghost of McFarland Leary." The name rolled off of David's tongue as if he were introducing the ghoul. "It's the perfect setup, especially since a lot of people around here still believe that Leary was responsible for the original murders."

"It's bloodcurdling."

He took her hands in his. "I don't want you to leave the house unless I know where you're going and unless I know you're properly protected. And if I'm not here to protect you, then Richard will be in charge."

"Why wouldn't you be here?"

"Because if Megham has his way, I'll be in jail, at least for questioning."

Fear, dread, anger—a collage of emotions she didn't begin to understand—collided inside her. "It's like the fairy tale where the prejudiced mob comes after the beast just because they don't understand him. And you're not a beast at all. They are. Megham is."

"I'm not a murderer. As long as you know that I can live with what Megham thinks."

"I know you'd never even hurt anyone, at least not intentionally." She buried her head against his chest, wrapped her arms around his waist and held on tight as he rocked her to him. Up until a few days ago, David Bryson had been the intriguing stranger on the hill, a man who'd stalked her mind by day and haunted her dreams at night.

Now he'd become her protector. And still she wanted more. No matter what danger lay outside the stone fence and guarded gate, she wanted David Bryson in her life.

CLAIRE CAVENDISH TOSSED and turned in her sleep as the habitual nightmare claimed her mind and body. The tomb was black, moldy, the putrid odor of decay clutching her every breath. Spiderwebs brushed across her face and adhered to her eyelashes, a gossamer veil that refused to be whisked away.

Someone grabbed her from behind, the way she knew he would, the way he always did. He clasped his hand over her mouth, silencing her scream, as the smell of whiskey burned her nostrils and mixed with the horror that heaved inside her.

She tried to break away, but he picked her up. A second later, they disappeared into the cold, narrow pathway that tunneled beneath the rocks and ended up out near the cliffs. When they exited, a gust of wind tore at her hair and plastered it against her face. It picked up the leaves and tossed them into a whirlwind of motion, the sudden gale moaning its way around the rocks, the desolate sound of the foghorn blaring in the distance.

Her friends were back at the cemetery, in their circle, holding hands. They would never know what had happened to her, never know that she'd been stolen from the mausoleum by the devil himself and taken straight to hell.

Claire woke with a start, her breath so shallow and fast, she felt as if she were suffocating. She knew at once it was only the dream, but something was different. She'd covered new ground, gone deeper into the recesses of her memory than she'd ever gone before.

She tried to think back. There had to be something about the man that would identify him. A voice. A smell. Something in his touch.

But there was nothing. Even though she'd finally got past the first horrible moment of contact, her mind was still protecting her from the full truth of what had happened during the time she'd been with the monster.

Kicking back the tangled sheets, she stretched her feet to the floor, flicked on the lamp by her bed and reached for her diary. She had to write everything down while it was fresh in her mind. Some people might say it was just a dream, that it meant nothing.

Claire was convinced it was much more. It was her way back to the living. Once she knew who had stolen her youth and her mind, once he was behind bars, she'd at least have a chance of moving past the dread that seemed to suck the very life from her.

She wished she could talk to Becca again, but Becca had moved into the Bluffs, moved in with a man who might not even be human. ''Take care, Becca,'' she whispered into the quiet of the night. ''Please take care of yourself.''

ONCE DETECTIVE MEGHAM LEFT, David had gone straight to his lab and stayed there for the rest of the afternoon. But, for the first time since Becca had moved into the Bluffs, he had joined her for dinner. Richard had gone into town, saying he had plans for the evening, but she knew he was giving them time to be alone.

They'd both avoided talk of serial killers and security

and finding the body. Instead, they chose topics more favorable to digestion. The weather and the house itself.

Right after dinner, David had disappeared again and she hadn't seen him since. Now, bathed and dressed in her prettiest nightshirt, she sat on the edge of the bed and thumbed through a copy of *National Geographic*. And the file on Joyce Telatia that she'd found in David's library found its way into her mind.

Why would David have collected so much material on a woman who'd been killed twenty years ago? And what had spawned his fascination with murders and serial killers, prompted him to fill the shelves of his library with books on the subject? Surely, there was some logical explanation.

Or was there the slightest chance that she was truly *bewitched* by a phantom or perhaps a mortal with two completely different personalities? One—a man who was tortured by loss. The other—a man who could kill in cold blood and show no remorse. And if that were true, did he even suspect the truth about himself?

"Becca."

She jumped to a sitting position at the sound of David's voice.

"I noticed your light was on and thought I'd stop in and say good-night. I hope I didn't wake you."

"No, I was just looking at a magazine." She tossed the *National Geographic* to the bedside table.

"Do you mind if I come in?"

"It's late."

"True, but you're awake, and so am I." His voice was like a silken spray, covering her from head to toe, caressing. He sat down on the edge of the bed beside her. "You're beautiful, Becca. So young." His fingers trailed her face. "So soft."

The fears from a few minutes ago surfaced, then drowned in the desire that coursed through her as David's fingers trailed a path down her neck, to the exposed cleavage at her collar. "I tried to stay away from you. I just can't. I've wanted to make love to you since the first night I saw you."

"Why me, David? I'm just a seamstress. A nobody. Why do you want me?"

"I've asked myself that question a thousand times. All I know is that you've taken over my mind and my will. You're all I can think about."

And then his lips were on hers. Soft, coaxing, then growing hard and demanding. But his hunger was no more than her own as he eased her back to the bed, then lifted her feet to the top of the quilt and stretched out beside her. He kissed her forehead, her eyelids, her cheeks, as his fingers worked the buttons loose on her nightshirt.

Her body was on fire now, flashes of intense heat and desire so strong it took her breath away. Her hands roamed his shoulders and back as her nightshirt fell open and she lay totally exposed to David's mouth and hands and eyes.

His fingers raked across her breasts and past her waist. "You're so perfect. So beautiful. Just lie back and let me make love to you, Becca."

She couldn't have refused had she wanted to, and she didn't want to. Her body craved him, her mind so possessed by him that she felt as if they were already one.

She moaned softly as his fingers skimmed the curves of her body, lingering over each breast, making her nipples pebble-hard before taking them in his mouth one by one. And then his hands splayed across her stomach, his thumbs moving in concentric circles, stirring her so that her insides seemed to be melting.

She arched to him as he lowered his mouth to her body and sent her spiraling to the top, then over the edge. She moaned in sweet relief and tried to catch her breath as her heart thundered inside her chest.

"Did you like it?" David whispered when she cuddled against him, content in the afterglow.

"I loved it." And still her words were an understatement. It was like nothing she'd ever experienced before. "Now it should be your turn." She tangled her fingers in the buttons of his shirt.

"Not tonight."

His words were uneven, scratchy, as if he were trying desperately to tamp down the same desires that had driven her wild just a few seconds earlier. She started to push for an explanation, then stopped and grew cold at the possibility that flooded her mind.

He'd been in a terrible explosion. He'd lost part of his face, but what else had he lost? The idea that he could never make love again felt like weights on her chest, crushing her lungs.

"Don't look so horrified, Becca. I told you. I've learned to live with the life fate's handed me. But I won't expose you to such a sight."

"Is that all you're talking about, just some burned flesh that you think is unattractive? Is that the reason you won't make love to me all the way?"

"It's reason enough."

"Not for me, David. And it shouldn't be for you. I don't care what you look like. I care about us."

He jerked to a standing position and looked down at her, his face hardened into lines of granite, his dark eyes as piercing as a sword. "Okay, Becca. You win. And once again, I'm going to lose."

In one frantic motion, he jerked his shirt open, the buttons tearing loose and bouncing across the floor. "Look at me, Becca, and then tell me you'd ever want to make love with a man who looks like this."

Becca gasped, then averted her gaze, hating herself for not being able to hide the initial shock. Once the shock abated, it wasn't repulsion she felt but an overwhelming sense of sadness for the pain David must have suffered and the anguish he felt now.

He clutched the shirt with both hands and jerked it back together, covering the ribbed area of pinkish, curdled flesh that swept across his belly. "So you see, the people in town were right all along. I am a beast." He hesitated, then looked up and let his gaze lock with hers. "I'm sorry, Becca. For everything."

His apology ground inside her, tearing at her like a vicious cat might tear at its prey. "A burn like that must have hurt terribly," she said, trying desperately to keep her voice on a steady keel.

"It did. But that was the kind of pain that pills could help. Looking in the mirror every day hurts far more."

"I'm sure you've seen a plastic surgeon."

"Several. Grafting new skin is a long, painful process at best. I haven't had the best. My body rejects a lot of the grafts and I've had serious problems with bacterial infections following many of the surgeries. It seems that after all the work on my face, my body has just decided it's had enough for a while. The doctors are optimistic that over time they can make me less of a ghoul, but there are no guarantees."

"There are no guarantees about any part of life, David. Not for you, or me, and there certainly were none for the two women who were brutally murdered. But as long as we're alive, we have to keep fighting.''

"So they say." He turned away but stopped and leaned one hand against the door frame, his head hung low, the defeat weighing down every part of his body.

"Don't go, David. Please, don't go."

"Stay and see you pity me? Watch you try to make yourself touch me when the very sight of me makes you sick to your stomach? No thanks."

"Then go. Sit by yourself and wallow in self-pity. You obviously don't have a clue how I feel, anyway."

"Are you saying the sight of my mangled skin doesn't repulse you?" It was more of a challenge than a question.

"It's ugly and it's unfortunate. But I'd want you, David Bryson, even if you sprouted green antennae or an extra nose."

He shook his head, his expression reflecting just how incredible he thought her reaction. "How could you possibly want me to stay after what you've just seen?"

"It's simple. I love you." She hadn't meant to say the words, but they'd slipped out, and now that she'd said them, she was glad. She did love him, and she was certain she'd never wanted any man the way she wanted him right now.

He turned back to her, still clutching his shirt so that the worst of his stomach was covered. "I have nothing to offer a woman like you, Becca."

"I didn't say it was smart or right to love you. I only said that I do." She stood and took a few steps, stopping just in front of him. Fitting her fingers around the edges of the front placket, she pushed the shirt open.

"You don't have to do this."

"I do. I have to do it for me. I can't pick and choose

parts of you to love.'' She splayed her hands across the wound, amazed how easy it was to do. Awed by the fact that desire coursed through her with the power of an ocean current.

He shuddered at her touch, and when she looked up at him, his eyes were closed tight, moisture pooling in the corners. And then he wrapped his arms around her and his lips found hers. He picked her up and carried her to the bed, laying her down in the center of it before climbing in beside her.

He kissed her mouth, her face, her eyes, then trailed downward and buried his lips in the hollow of her neck. As always his kisses set her on fire.

They made love in a frenzied tangling of arms and legs and heated touches that left her breathless. The dreams of him had been erotic beyond anything she could have imagined, but feeling him inside her was a million times more exciting. They came together with a hunger so intense, she forgot explosions and killers and danger.

All she knew was that she was finally one with David. And it was perfect.

THE WHOLE ATMOSPHERE of the Bluffs changed after that night of making love. In spite of the danger lurking all around, in spite of the knowledge that Megham was probably working on getting an arrest warrant, in spite of the body of the killer's latest victim being found on the grounds, David seemed more relaxed than at any point since she'd met him.

She wasn't sure if it was the actual act of consummation—as glorious as it was—that had made the difference in him or if it was the fact that he'd gotten past showing her the damaged flesh that he'd thought would totally repulse her. Whatever the reason for his change in mood, she couldn't help but smile as she sat across the dinner table in the cozy garden room.

"Will you be working in the lab tonight?" she asked, when David had finished the last morsel of chocolate cake.

"No. I plan to spend the next few hours going over some notes and files."

She swirled the last few drops of coffee in her cup, then finished it. "What kind of old notes?"

"Pieces to a puzzle that never quite fit."

"I take it you don't mean an actual jigsaw puzzle."

"No. A twenty-year-old murder mystery. A mad bomber. Records of doctors with sick minds."

"Why such an interest in a murder that took place twenty years ago."

"The whole town's curious, as are the multitude of tourists who flock here every year. Why wouldn't I be?"

"It just doesn't seem like you."

"You're right. I'm interested in Joyce Telatia and the other victims because I think there's a chance they could be connected to the explosion that killed Tasha."

She found his answer incredible. "How would they be connected?"

"There are things that have gone on in this town for twenty years, illegal, immoral, unethical things, and they involve some of the most upstanding citizens. Some have been uncovered, but not all. A lot of people still have a tremendous amount to lose."

"Is this connected to the secret medical society that we talked about before?"

"Possibly. It's a tangled maze, but I can't go pointing fingers without facts to back them up."

"Who do you think is behind it?"

"This isn't fit after-dinner conversation, Becca, and there's no reason for you to take on these problems when you already have so much to deal with. When the killer is caught and your life has settled down again, I'll fill you in on the details, that is, if you're still interested. Now, I suggest we finish our coffee before it gets cold. I still have work to do tonight."

She tried to make light conversation, but the mood had been destroyed. But she stayed at the table after David finished and left, nursing a cup of lukewarm coffee and trying to imagine what possible connection the unsolved murders of twenty years ago could have on Tasha's death.

Some people in town believed David had killed those three women. Some probably believed he was the madman serial killer who'd killed the two women in the last few days. Others would be sure it was McFarland Leary himself or some deranged psychotic who thought himself to be Leary.

Finally she left the table and walked the long hall to the staircase that led to the library where she had first seen the file. She spent the next hour perusing copies of book on true crime and medical and psychiatric studies on the minds of serial killers. The material was chilling, and she shivered as she stopped in front of the one bookcase she hadn't looked at before.

She pulled out a heavy volume. Her fingernail brushed a bump at the back of the bookcase. Stooping, she looked to see what she'd touched and saw a smooth black knob. She hesitated for only a second before she pushed it. A second later the bookshelves slid apart and a wooden door appeared.

Hands shaking, she opened the door and stared into a dark tunnel that disappeared into total blackness. A million questions swam in her mind. Serial killers, Joyce Telatia, rumors that David Bryson was a madman who killed innocent women in cold blood, even his fiancée.

Questions without answers. Only she had the strange idea that the answers might all be waiting at the end of the tunnel. She looked around the room, spotted a gas lantern and a book of matches. All the light she'd need, for as long as she'd need it. Unless she never returned.

The echo of her footsteps seemed deafening as she made her way down a series of dark steps and through tomblike passages. If there was such a thing as ghosts, they would surely be at home here. Her foot bumped against something that bounced off the wall and went careering down the passageway. When she got close enough, she lowered her light and saw the eerie glow of the flickering flames creeping over a skull. She swallowed the scream, but it rattled inside her head, nearly driving her wild. And still she kept walking.

Finally, the passageway widened. Stopping beneath an arched doorway, she took in her first view of a rambling system of columns and arches that extended far beneath the Bluffs. It was a basement of sorts, though like no basement she'd ever seen before. She was standing in an open area about the size of the ballroom, but a series of meandering hallways ran off in every direction.

She had no idea which path to take, so she just started walking down the first dark passage. It intersected with other corridors, and after a couple of turns, she realized that she might not be able to find her way out.

Fear ran icy fingers up her spine and along the back of her neck. Maybe this had originally been a tomb. That would explain the skull. Or maybe it had been more of a dungeon, with people locked down here while they were still alive and left to wander the dark, cold corridors until they became so weak they just passed out and eventually died.

She forced her feet and legs to keep moving forward, though she felt like Claire must have felt the other night when they'd almost been attacked near her house. Her insides quivered, and she could have easily dissolved into a formless heap.

And then she saw a light. A few feet ahead, a ribbon of light around what appeared to be the outline of a door. She stopped, but the soft echo of footsteps still sounded behind her.

She wasn't alone.

Chapter Fifteen

"Are you looking for something?"

Becca swung around and found Richard only a few feet behind her. The darkness and shadows changed his appearance, gave his skin an eerie glow and turned his hair the color of soured cream.

"I'm looking for David," she lied, amazed that in this setting even Richard seemed threatening.

"Then you've come to the right place. Just follow the light. Open the door and you'll find him."

She did as he said, stepping into a room that had been set up as an office. A half-dozen oil lamps had been strategically placed around the room, all of them burning. There was a folding card table set up in the middle of the room, two folding metal chairs, a laptop computer, and boxes of books, files and disks stacked everywhere. All things that could have been carried through the narrow passageway that she'd just followed.

David sat at a table, a file open in front of him. Seventy rooms inside the Bluffs and he had made this dark chamber inside the catacombs his office.

"How did you find me?" David asked, peering at her over the back of the folder.

"I was looking at books in the library and I accidentally touched the button that parted the bookcases."

"Pure luck."

He didn't specify if it was good or bad luck, and at this point, she hadn't decided, either. David definitely didn't appear to be overjoyed to see her.

"I didn't know where the passage would wind up."

"But you decided to follow it, anyway. You are a very brave woman, Becca. It's a miracle you found me at all. If you hadn't made the correct turns, you might have been lost down here for days, or months, with no one even knowing to look for you here."

But she'd made the right turns, almost without thinking, as if someone, or some *thing* had been guiding her here. It was too creepy for words.

"I brought the files you asked for," Richard said, from his position by the door. "Would you like me to walk Becca back into the house as I go?"

"No. She's here now. She may as well know everything."

She wandered closer, letting her gaze scan the folders on the table. Dr. Leland Manning's name jumped up at her. "Why would you work down here, David, when you have such a beautiful home to work in?"

"For years it was the only place I felt comfortable. I didn't use it as an office until recently, but now, it seems appropriate for the tasks I perform here."

She leaned against the folding table that David was using as a desk. "The puzzle that you said you were trying to solve?"

He spread his hands as if encompassing the entire array of files spread across his desk. "These are printouts of Leland Manning's files. Most of them have to do with his connection to the secret society. I'm convinced the missing piece of the puzzle is somewhere in these notes.''

"How did you get Manning's notes? I'd have thought the police would have taken them when they arrested him.''

"I stole them before the police had a chance to confiscate them.'' He stood and pulled out a chair for her. "Have a seat and I'll tell you what I've learned so far. But let me warn you that it's as grim and as demonic as any nightmare known to man.''

"Like the nightmare Claire lived through.''

"Every bit as heinous. In fact, I wouldn't be at all surprised if Claire's abduction and torture aren't connected to our original killer. It would fit his pattern perfectly—only Claire escaped before he'd finished what he'd started.''

She dropped into the chair, her insides knotted into a tight ball, her heart pumping in overtime. Last night she'd lain in David's arms, flushed with pleasure and heated by the afterglow of making love. Today she was in a web of cold, dark chambers.

David reached over and took her hand. "You're pale, Becca. Maybe we should just go back. I don't want to frighten you.''

"No, I'd like to hear what you discovered in the notes. I'm already involved in this and I'd like to know what I'm up against.''

"Whatever you're up against, the man isn't going to win. Not this time. We are.''

And once again she believed him and loved him so much that the fear dried up like a hot sidewalk after a summer rain. "Let's hear it,'' she said. "I can handle it.''

"Then let's start with this.''

He pulled a small, worn book from a desk drawer and handed it to her. The fabric that held the lock had decayed and frayed. She tucked her finger under the cover and lifted it, studying the handwritten note on page one. *The diary of Joyce Telatia.* Her hands began to shake.

"Where did you get this?"

"From Leland Manning's office. Just jump to the back, starting about a dozen pages from the end. The entry in question is highlighted."

She read the first sentence of the marked passage. *I met a fascinating young man today, and I feel totally bewitched.*

SHAMUS MCMANUS SAT at the end of the bar, swigging down his whiskey on the rocks and listening to the acrimonious grumbling going on all around him. Two murders in a week's time. Both young women. Both found naked with their jugular veins cut. Everyone had a theory, but no one knew jack about what had really happened. Least of all the police.

"Hey, Shamus, you got an alibi for the time of the murders? That old relic detective they've got on the case is questioning everybody in town, and a grouchy old buzzard like you is sure to be on the list."

He stared at the man asking the questions—Sammy Jacobs—stained sweatshirt, tobacco-stained lips, his beer belly punching into the bar.

"I don't need an alibi. If I were going to kill someone, it wouldn't be young, good-looking women. It would be an old cuss like you that the world wouldn't even miss."

"Wasn't a man that killed them," Marley Glasglow said. "It was Leary. The police are trying to keep it quiet, but I know someone who works at the morgue and he's heard plenty."

Kevin Pinelle straddled the bar stool next to Marley. "Right on, Marley. Why don't you and me just go to the cemetery and take care of that bag of bones?"

Marley turned and stared at Kevin. "Everything's a joke to you, isn't it, pretty boy? I wouldn't be surprised to find you lying naked one night with your throat slit."

The bartender turned from the mug he was filling with draft beer. "Yeah, but it will probably be because some guy found him in bed with his wife."

A few guys laughed, but nothing like the guffaws that would have filled the room on a regular night. The murders had cut into the serenity of the small coastal town, the fear sticky and thick as the fog blowing in tonight. The mood was getting to Shamus.

He heard the door open behind him and felt the draft as a burst of cold air slunk inside. When he looked up, he caught a glimpse of Marley's face. It was white as a sheet.

Sammy jumped to his feet. "What the hell!"

Shamus turned around to see a man in the door. A McFarland Leary mask covered his face, topped by a stringy white wig.

Kevin burst out laughing. "Larry Gayle, you are one crazy man."

Larry jerked the mask from his face. "How did you know it was me?"

"You got on the shirt you had on at lunch today. Ketchup stains right in the same place."

The foghorn sounded in the distance and Shamus knew the fog would be rolling in, thick, blanketing the coast like a shroud. A perfect night for McFarland Leary to be on the prowl.

BLOOD WAS ON HIS MIND as the man walked the area along the wharf. Up until a week ago, he'd imagined that the sight of warm blood spurting from a dying person would be nauseating. Now it was all he could think about.

But he had decided to kill only three women, and that's the way it had to be. It would be the crime spree of the century, relived over and over again in stories told to the tourists when they visited Moriah's Landing.

One more to go. Becca Smith. Beautiful, with her shiny blond hair, her shapely body, her tinkling laugh. But it would all come to an end when he took the sharp blade of the knife and sliced through the jugular. Quick and simple.

But that was all that would be simple about her murder. Her moving into the Bluffs had complicated everything else. But the details were all worked out. The flower delivery van made a trip to the walled-in fortress once a week. This time he'd be in it, stowed away in the back beneath the blankets used when transporting the large glass swans they used for weddings.

But there would be nothing in the back of the panel van when they delivered David Bryson's white roses. There never was. The driver made the long trip to the Bluffs early, before the other deliveries were ready. And the long white boxes of roses rode in the passenger seat, right next to the driver. He knew. He'd checked out all the details.

While the driver walked to the house with the flowers, he'd sneak out of the van and find a nice place to hide until the time was right. The Bluffs was a huge place with lots of windows and doors. And one would lead to Becca. By this time tomorrow night, her body would have been found and safely ensconced in the morgue.

He'd be in the bar having a beer with the talk of

murder all around him. He'd be infamous. Too bad no one but him would ever know.

BECCA FINISHED READING the diary and laid it on the table. It was obvious that in the days before Joyce Telatia's murder, she'd been involved in some sort of bizarre, secret research project. It was also obvious that she'd become obsessed with some man whom she didn't identify.

"Who do you think the young man was that Joyce was in love with?"

"From the description, I'd say it was Leland Manning, which would explain how he came to get his hands on her diary before the police did."

"I read the accounts of the murders in the newspaper files. There was no mention of Leland's having dated Joyce."

"I'm sure they didn't date. Leland was married at the time, but there must have been some kind of affair going on between them, one the cops never heard about."

"Lots of men have affairs, David. That doesn't make them murderers."

"True, but there is no record of any projects involving students at that particular time. That's why I think the secret society might have been behind the projects. Joyce became involved, and she was murdered."

"But the newspaper indicated the killings were all random."

"They may have been, a random selection of young women involved in the project. I was investigating the secret society at the time my boat blew up. I think it was someone trying to get rid of me before I found out too much. Only it wasn't me they killed. It was Tasha." Sadness turned his eyes into a pool of dark chocolate.

As always, everything in David's life eventually came back to Tasha. It shouldn't hurt, but it did. Every time she made a step forward with him, Tasha's name came up and it seemed she fell two steps back.

"What have you learned from Manning's notes?" she asked, preferring to concentrate on something she might be able to help with.

"In the beginning, the society was more of a social club, a place where men got together to play poker, drink whiskey and discuss the topical events of the day, especially those related to the medical field. It was made up mostly of local doctors, but there were always a few key business people in the group, as well." He rummaged through his notes. "Take a look at this."

He spent the next two hours showing her the basics of what he'd discovered after months of scrutinizing Manning's notes. Some of the society members had become obsessed with the search to find the fountain of youth through research experiments using blood taken from direct descendants of women identified as witches in Moriah's Landing in the seventeenth century.

Although the research was far from conclusive, they had identified a gene that they referred to simply as "gene W," the witch gene. The goal was to clone new cells that included that gene, implant the new cells in humans and have it become a part of a living human's genetic makeup. What they hoped for was a human who didn't age in the traditional way. They were never successful, and apparently there was a lot of bickering among the members who were involved as to what was morally and legally acceptable research on live subjects and what wasn't.

The more Becca read, the more upset she became. She'd always held doctors in such high regard, but read-

ing the notes, she realized that a few had been willing
to completely ignore the Hippocratic oath for their own
mercenary and personal benefit.

If they had found the proverbial fountain of youth,
they would have not only dramatically increased their
own longevity, but in all likelihood would have become
unbelievably wealthy in the process, the way David had
when he'd made the major breakthrough in genetic research, discovered drugs that were now used in hospitals
and research centers around the globe. But for these
men, it was a matter of selling their souls to the devil.

"I think I've seen enough for one night," she said,
rubbing her eyes. "More than I ever wanted to know
about the corrupt side of medicine."

"It's pretty gruesome," he admitted.

"I'm still not sure why you're so certain that the murders were connected to the society."

"Not to the society as a whole, but to one person in
the society. It's that name I have to come up with. The
name and indisputable proof."

"It boggles the mind, and I'm too tired to think anymore tonight."

He straightened a stack of notes, walked over and put
his hands on her shoulders. His fingers dug into her flesh,
kneading her tired muscles. But as always, there was no
way for them to touch without the sparks igniting into
a full-blown fire. His thumbs traced the lines of her neck.

A second later she was in his arms, kissing him again
and again, the need swallowing up the sludge and mire
they'd waded through for the past dismal hours. She
ached to make love to him, but not in the catacombs,
not in a room where depravity was spread out on the
table like food for demons.

"Let's go back to my room," she said, breaking from the kiss.

"Not tonight."

Puzzled and hurt, she pulled away from him.

He fit his hands around her waist. "I think it's time you moved into the master suite with me."

"I can handle that."

Using the flashlight to guide their way, he led her back through the bleak catacombs, through the oppressively narrow passageway and to the steep steps. Skulls, skeletons, lost souls wandering endlessly in a world of darkness. The images assaulted her mind, but she refused to let them take hold.

"You're awfully quiet," David said. "I probably hit you with way too much information for one night."

"Nonsense. I'm a big girl."

"You're tough."

"Like you, I had to be if I wanted to survive. Besides, I was just imagining people being locked away down here without food or water."

"More likely it was used for storing goods that were imported illegally and then sold in the colonies. The Pierce who built the house originally was in the shipping business."

"The history of the Pierces and that of Moriah's Landing must be intertwined from the very beginning."

"Yes, I can just imagine a Pierce throwing the first stone at someone suspected of being a witch, or stringing up the rope to hang that witch."

"Strange how this town has kept its fascination with witches, warlocks, vampires and ghosts intact for three hundred and fifty years."

"I hated those tales when I was growing up. My earliest memories are of lying in my bed at night, listening to the wind howl through the trees or the blast of the foghorn, and I'd imagine it was the ghosts coming to get me. And on those nights when the fog rolled in so thick I couldn't even see the tree outside my window, I'd imagine it was poison spewing from the mouths of the witches that had been killed in the seventeenth century.''

''How old were you then?''

''Only four or five. I toughened up quick when I started school. I had to. The other kids knew what my mom did for a living and they never let me forget it.''

''But if you hated this town so much, why did you come back here?''

''The town wouldn't let me go.''

It was a bizarre comment, but in a way she understood it. The first day she'd come to Moriah's Landing, she'd felt as if it were reaching out to her, as if she belonged here. ''Did you know about the catacombs when you bought the house?'' she asked.

''No, but I found them shortly after, while Tasha and I were dating. We discovered a yellowed layout of the house in a rusted trunk at the back of the attic. I did the carpentry work myself, opened one passage, and put in the sliding bookcase to cover it.''

''A man of many talents.''

''And I plan to show you all of them.''

''Sounds intriguing.'' As everything about David did. ''How many people know the catacombs exist?''

''Aside from the original owner, I'm not certain, other than me and Richard and, of course, Tasha before she died. I've found human skulls and bones down here, as well as the skulls of animals, so I think they must have been used as a mausoleum of sorts at one time, or for some type of sacrificial ceremonies.''

"Let's just hope the sacrificial ceremonies were a long time ago."

"Probably a century or two. As for who else knows about the catacombs, I'm not even certain the current generation of Pierces knew about them, though you can still feel a draft if you stand near the openings that are boarded over."

"That explains the cold spots."

"I guess Richard told you about them."

"Yes, but he didn't mention the secret passage that we came through or the catacombs."

"Just one more corner, then we'll reach the exit that leads into the library."

She gulped in a deep breath as they stepped out of the passageway and into the light. And once again she was struck speechless by the sheer grandeur of the Bluffs. Perhaps it was the starkness of the catacombs she'd just left, but the massive chandelier, the hand-carved molding, the hand-painted ceiling over the library, the dark, rich wood of the bookcases seemed like something from a fairy tale as her feet sank into the thickness of the Persian rug.

"I love this room," she said. "The books and the warmth of the wood. It think it's my favorite in the whole house, at least of the ones I've seen."

He looked around as if seeing the room for the first time. "It was Tasha's favorite room, too. She used to come in here to study for her classes at the university."

Tasha. Yet again. She was sorry she'd said she liked the room now. And once again she wondered if she'd ever be able to compete with the memory of a woman who hadn't lived long enough to ever do anything wrong.

"You seem so quiet," David said. "Have I done something to upset you?"

"Not intentionally. It's just that what we have doesn't seem enough to compete with your memories."

"That's not true. It's just…"

David walked to the window, pushed back the heavy drape and stared out into the darkness. Things had been going so well a minute ago, now they were crumbling around him. The last person in the world he wanted to hurt was Becca. What he wanted to do was protect her, hold her, drown in her kisses. So why couldn't he just move on and let the past go? He knew Tasha would want him to.

She stepped behind him. "Finish the sentence, David. It's just what? That I'm not Tasha? That I'll never be her? You can say it. I may not like it, but I won't go ape on you."

He struggled to find the right words to explain feelings he didn't understand. "It's just that I've lived on memories for so long. I never expected to have another chance at love, never thought anyone could desire this mangled mess of a body. I guess it's just all happening too fast for me to adjust. I know Tasha would want me to go on, and yet I feel almost as if I'm betraying her."

"Then don't betray her, David. Stay here and live on your memories. Love her as much as you like for as long as you like, but she isn't coming back. And I can't stay with you knowing that I'll never come first with you."

He heard her footsteps as she walked away, ached to run after her and hold her so close he could feel her heart beating against his chest. Longed to make love with her over and over again. But he couldn't, not until he knew he could deliver what she asked. He owed that not only to Becca, but to himself.

He started to walk to the locked room where he went so often on lonely nights. The one place he still felt close to Tasha. A few feet down the corridor, he changed his mind. Nothing would give him peace tonight. So he might as well drive into town and see what he could discover about the town's reaction to the latest murder.

And, if miracles still happened, he might even find out something that would give him the identity of the killer. But he wouldn't lurk in the shadows. Not anymore. Those days were over.

If his experience with Becca had taught him nothing else, it was that he was a lot more than flesh and blood, and if people didn't like the way he looked, that was their problem. And if they didn't like the fact that he was the owner of the Bluffs now, well, that was their problem, too.

Moving almost silently, he let himself out the front door, careful to lock it behind him. The security was all in place. Becca would be safe. And protection might be the only good and decent thing he could give her.

DAVID COULD HEAR the din of laughter, loud talk and the jarring blast of the jukebox a half block before he reached the door of Wheels. Within seconds after he pushed his way inside, the talking and laughter stopped, leaving only the blare of the jukebox to fill the void. He let his gaze travel the smoky saloon, looking one man after another in the eye before finally walking to the bar and sliding onto a barstool between Shamus McManus and a bearded man he didn't recognize.

Shamus was the first one to break the silence. "Are you lost, Bryson?"

"Not likely. I grew up on the wharf, remember."

"Oh, I remember well. I took you on your first fishing trip and taught you how to drive your mom's old Chevy. You're the one who seems to have forgotten where you came from."

"I've got my memory back now." He stared at the bartender. "What's a man have to do to get a drink around here?"

The bartender wiped his hands on his apron but stayed his distance. "You're not welcome in here, Bryson."

"You got a policy against serving scientists?"

"I have a policy against serving murderers."

"If you have any kind of evidence against me, then call the cops and have me arrested. Otherwise, I'll have a whiskey on the rocks. And one for my friend Shamus."

"I told you you're not welcome."

Shamus banged his glass down on the table so hard that a piece of the ice shot out and bounced across the bar. "Hell. Ain't none of us welcome in here. You just like our money, and Bryson's got more of it than any of the rest of us. Now, pour the blasted drinks before I come behind the bar and do it for you. And the rest of you in here…" He raised his voice so that it boomed over the jukebox. "This is David Bryson. Used to be the roughest, brattiest kid on the wharf. Back then he had a right hook that would set your head rattling for days. I hear it's worse now, so if you want to tangle with him, I suggest you pay your insurance up first. If not, then quit gawking and get back to your drinkin'."

The bartender poured the drinks and set them in front of them. There were a few grumbles at the back of the room and a lot of stares, but the noise level increased and a guy pulled a shapely redhead into his arms and started doing moves that David guessed passed for dancing.

"You always were quite an orator," David said, clinking his glass with Shamus's.

"And you always had piss-poor timing. So what the devil are you doing making your grand entrance at the same time we got us another serial killer making the rounds?"

"Like you said. I've got piss-poor timing. Now, have you got any ideas who's behind the murders?"

"A couple, though I've got nothing but speculation to go on. Finish your drink and we'll go back to my place where we can talk."

IT WAS NEARLY TWO WHEN DAVID drove the winding road back to the Bluffs. He hadn't learned much from Shamus, but tonight had still been an important milestone for him. He'd stepped back into the world of the living, not tentatively, but boldly, and he'd done it without covering the scar on his face.

He'd made another decision tonight, too. He prayed he'd made the right one.

THE WHITE PANEL VAN ROCKED and rattled along Old Mountain Road. By the time the driver slowed for the turn onto the private road to the Bluffs, his hidden passenger was impatient and trying hard not to sneeze. The blanket was scratchy with a sickeningly sweet flower smell that made him feel as if he were awake for his own funeral.

One more murder. One more knife slicing across the neck. Quick and simple. This time he wouldn't even stay around to hide the body. He'd just scatter the vial of dirt he'd brought from Leary's grave over the body and then he'd be gone. Back through the woods and over the fence.

He could pick even the best of locks with the speed of Houdini. A teenage career of breaking and entering had taught him that.

His heart rate increased. This would be his last murder—for a while, anyway. He'd miss it, the act itself and the satisfaction of knowing he could do it and never get caught. Not to mention the fun of watching those idiots in town speculating whether or not a ghost was popping off their young women.

The van jerked to a stop. Evidently they were at the gate. He could hear the driver punching in the secret codes that opened it. The man didn't breathe easy until the van jerked forward—at least as easy as a man could breathe buried under a pile of blankets with only a tiny space between him and the wall to grab some oxygen.

Jump from the truck while the driver made the delivery. Hide in the row of shrubs that bordered the walk to the garden and then make a run for cover. Lucky for David Bryson he'd have a fresh supply of white roses to scatter over his newest dead girlfriend.

Chapter Sixteen

Becca hurried toward a front window when she heard the doorbell ring, hoping it wasn't Detective Megham again. It wasn't. It was the deliveryman from the florist. She couldn't see his truck, but she recognized the ribbon-tied boxes that the roses came in. White roses to be scattered over the cliffs in memory of Tasha Pierce.

The first time she'd witnessed it, she'd found the practice endearing. Today it only assured her that she'd made the right decision. As soon as she found a place to go, she'd be leaving the Bluffs.

Even if David convinced her to stay, it wouldn't work. Every time she caught him staring into space or looking as if his mind were a million miles away, she'd always wonder if it was Tasha who was on his mind. When they kissed, she'd worry that it was Tasha he was thinking of. When they made love, she'd… She had to stop this. It was making her physically ill.

But maybe she was being too hard on David, expecting too much too soon. Just because she'd fallen so hard, so fast, didn't mean he would have the same reaction. Given time, he might be able to let Tasha slide into the background and love Becca as much as she loved him.

She walked down the hall and trudged the steep staircase, drawn to his shrine to Tasha. Pausing outside the door, she closed her eyes and imagined Tasha in the beautiful wedding gown, her eyes shining with love, her heart overflowing. Tears burned at the back of Becca's eyelids as she walked away. She and Tasha had so much in common. They had both lost their hearts to David. But Tasha still possessed him.

Becca walked down one long hallway after another, not caring where she went, as long as it was away from that room. She had no idea how far she'd walked or exactly where she was, but finally she stopped and leaned against the wall and tried to get her bearings. She was fairly certain she hadn't been in this part of the house before, but all of a sudden she had the creepy feeling that she wasn't alone. She turned and looked down the hall behind her.

"Who's there?"

There was no answer and not a sign of movement. Paranoia was catching up with her. There were always noises in a place this old. She opened a door and stepped into a windowless rectangular room with chairs and folded tables stacked along the wall. An antique dining table, covered with a leather pad, sat directly beneath a brass chandelier, as if ruling over the clutter.

A large cardboard box rested in the middle of the table, the edges folded back, revealing the top half of a skull and a hand that seemed to be scratching and clawing its way out of the container. A gob of white hair poked from around the skull, tumbling over the rim of the box like a clump of spiderwebs.

Just Halloween decorations, she told herself. But still her stomach constricted then rolled inside her as she walked to the table. Her hands shook and she could feel a drop of cold sweat sliding between her breasts as she reached inside the box, wrapped her hands around the wig and pulled.

The hideous rubber mask of McFarland Leary fell against her, the blank eyes staring at her. She went weak and the room spun around her like a carousel gone mad.

Get a grip, Becca. It's nothing but stupid decorations. Lots of people own these ridiculous masks. Holding the edge of the table, she struggled for a deep breath and some equilibrium.

Instead she heard the sound of the door behind her closing and the lock clicking into place. She spun around. The first thing she saw was the pointed blade of a knife. The second was the face of the man holding the knife.

"Hello, Becca. Time to meet the real beast."

Becca stared at the man, knowing she'd seem him before but unable to remember where. "Who are you?"

"That's right, we haven't had the benefit of formal introductions, have we? His lips twisted into a taunting grin. "My friends call me Kevin. Most of the women just call me darlin'."

"Until you kill them?"

"That's right, sweetheart. Usually I give them the pleasure of my company first. Too bad I don't have time to do that for you. A stuck-up broad like you could use the attention of a man like me."

The thought of his hands on her, much less any other part of his body, made her skin crawl, but the thought of the knife slicing through her neck overrode everything else. The chances that someone would hear her scream were almost nil. And once she screamed, he'd waste no time in killing her.

There had to be a better way. "Why are you doing this?" she asked, trying to buy time to think.

"I'm just delivering what the town of Moriah's Landing wants. Think how disappointed they'd have been if old McFarland Leary hadn't come crawling out of his grave to kill off a few maidens. One here. One there. All inching closer to the monster on the hill. Now, this one will be right under his nose. Who'd ever convince a jury he's not the murderer?"

The man was horribly sick, and yet he'd planned the whole thing amazingly well. And she'd played right into his hands by moving into the Bluffs. She'd be dead. David would be in jail—for murders he'd never committed.

Unless…

Her gazed scanned the room. A skull, a mask, a horrid fake hand. All gruesome, but nothing that could help her now. She took a step backward, to the stack of folding chairs. "All this to set up David. Do you even know him?"

"It's not about David Bryson or even about you, sweetheart, though you've made a fascinating prospect from the night I decided to add you to the victim list."

She leaned her backside against a metal chair, putting her hands behind her and wrapping her fingers around the curved edge of the high back. "When was that?"

"The night you showed up at Wheels with Larry Gayle and those other two friends of yours. You shouldn't have dumped my buddy for the mad scientist. It wasn't cool."

"But even before that, you'd killed one woman and planned to lay the blame on David."

"That's right. You just added the whipped cream to my pie. A murderous ghost, a vampire in a Gothic castle, and a beautiful blond-haired woman who obviously has the hots for the beast. It's classic."

"And I made it easy for you by moving in with David?"

"Easy and difficult. The Cavendish home would have been much easier to break into than a stone fortress."

He laughed, not loud, yet the sound roared inside Becca's head. His left hand opened and closed, and the veins in his neck stood out like blue cords as he positioned the knife to attack. Images flew through her mind. The wedding dress and veil. Only she was wearing it, not Tasha. And she was dancing with David on the deck of the ship with a blanket of dazzling stars shining above them.

She and David. Making love and loving. Always, she and David.

Adrenaline rushed through her in a crushing wave and she pulled the chair from behind her and slung it at Kevin. It glanced off his chest, but it slowed him just long enough for her to grab another chair. She was screaming now, a piercing yell that reverberated from the ceiling and walls, screaming and swinging the chair like a club.

But the man just kept coming, the knife outstretched and ready to plunge into her neck and rip through her jugular just as he'd done with the other victims. He yanked the chair from her hands and hurled it across the room. She grabbed another for one last chance. This time she hammered the leg of the chair into his eyeball. He stumbled backward, but only for a minute.

When he recovered, he came at her like an angered bull, the muscles in his arms flexed into hard knots, blood pouring from the injured eye. He slapped her hard across the face, knocking her to the floor. Her head banged against the base of the table, blurring her vision and searing her body with pain.

When she looked up, she saw two knives, both of them coming toward her. And then her head seemed to explode. She fell back as the first drops of warm blood gushed onto her blouse.

"I love you, David. I love you so much. I wish I could have been Tasha for you, but…"

The words died on her lips as she sank into an abyss that pain and heartbreak couldn't reach.

Chapter Seventeen

At first David thought the screams were the wind howling around the corners of the Bluffs, the way it had done so many times before. But he was in the closed-in passage, making his way back up from the catacombs. There was no way he would hear the wind.

Oh, God, no. It was Becca. He recognized the voice now. And someone else's. A male. Laughing like a madman. Head down to avoid colliding with the ceiling, he started running, trying desperately to figure out which room the cries were coming from.

Within seconds, he'd cleared the bookcase door and started down the long hallway. *One more scream. Please, Becca, be alive and give me one more scream so that I can find you.*

But the hallway had grown strangely silent. He rounded a corner and his heart slammed against his chest. There was no scream, but he could hear banging noises, a clucking and scraping as if furniture were bouncing off the walls.

He reached the door, tried the knob only once before snatching the pistol from its holder and shooting the lock off. His hand still on the trigger, he kicked the door open and stared into the face of Kevin Pinelle. Kevin's hand was on the knife. The knife was on Becca's neck.

"Drop the knife or I shoot."

"Nah. I'm not much for jail time. Wouldn't go well at all for a pretty boy like me. So, I'll just kill her and let you shoot."

David pulled the trigger.

THE BACK OF BECCA'S HEAD pounded like the heavy bass of a punk rock tune. She opened her eyes and looked into David's. "We've got to stop meeting like this."

He cradled her head in his arms. "I always heard that if you save a woman once, they expect you to do it over and over."

Her hand scraped across the front of her blouse and paused in the sticky dampness. "Is that blood?"

"Yes, but not yours, though it would have been if I'd been a second longer."

"Did you kill my attacker?"

"No, just wounded his knife hand. I wouldn't want him to miss out on his prison experience. Now, if you can stand to be moved, I'm going to carry you to the front of the house. You took a nasty blow to the back of your head."

"Anything you say, Dr. Bryson." She managed to move her head enough to scan the room. "Where is Kevin?"

"Megham and Richard are downstairs with him while they wait for the ambulance. The second ambulance. The first one will be yours, and this time I am not taking no for an answer."

She rested her throbbing head against his chest, thankful to be alive, thankful that the current murder spree was over, thankful that no more women would die at the madman's hands.

She wouldn't let herself think beyond that yet. She knew how much she loved David, but the near-death experience didn't change their relationship. Loving him would never be enough as long as his devotion to a dead lover came first.

A haunted castle. A tortured lover. A twisted and unhappy ending. Just like in an old Gothic novel.

Bewitched. And bittersweet.

THE DIAGNOSIS HAD BEEN a mild concussion, and by the second afternoon, Becca was restless and anxious to be released from the hospital. They'd already kept her an extra day, just as a precautionary measure, or so the doctor had said, but she'd definitely be going home today.

Home. Only she didn't really have one anymore. She'd already moved her things out of the Cavendish home, and one of the younger children had claimed her space. And she couldn't go back to the Bluffs knowing that David was still in love with Tasha. She was strong but not that strong.

With her options limited, Becca had decided to move into the motel on the edge of town while she looked for a place to rent. A small efficiency apartment would be adequate for her needs—something with a short lease. Once she'd finished the dresses she had already agreed to design and sew for the Fall Extravaganza, she planned to move away.

She'd miss her new friends—Brie, Kat, Elizabeth and Claire—the only real friends she could remember. But if she stayed, it would be sheer torture to look up and see the Bluffs every day, to know David was there and that she would never be the one he loved.

The loss hurt far more than the blow to the head, even more than the surgeries that had reconstructed her nose and her jaw following the incident five years ago. This time the pain buried itself so deep inside that it permeated every part of her, lived with her every second of the day. But, unlike David, she would move past the pain and enervating loss. One day, though she knew it wouldn't be anytime soon.

She looked up as the door to her room squeaked open and Brie Pierce stepped inside.

"Hello, Miss Town Heroine," Brie purred, sweeping across the room to hug her.

"Me? A heroine?"

"I should say. You practically singlehandedly caught the serial killer who was terrifying the whole town."

"I didn't catch him. If David Bryson had been a few seconds later, I'd be dead."

"But you slowed the guy down until David could get there. And the report I heard was that you got in a few good whacks with a metal chair, practically took his eye out."

She grimaced at the thought. "How is his eye? I hope I didn't blind him."

Brie shook her head, and her hair bounced around her shoulders. She looked different since she'd married the man destined to be Moriah's Landing's next mayor, more sophisticated, but that in no way diminished the glow love had painted in her eyes and her smile.

"I can't believe you're worried about that monster," Brie said, "not after what he did to those two poor women and almost did to you."

Becca straightened the sheet and propped up a little

higher in the hospital bed. "It was Kevin Pinelle who tried to attack Claire and me that night, too. He admitted it."

"Only because he thinks some shyster lawyer is going to get him off with an insanity plea."

"He hasn't admitted running me off the road that evening, though," Becca said. "It seems he would if he's behind it. Once a man's admitted to two murders and an attempted murder, you wouldn't think he'd bother to lie about running someone off the road."

"Drew's convinced he did it, though. He thinks Kevin's just trying to throw some suspicion on someone else, that he's the kind of guy who likes to keep the cops and news media jumping through his hoops. Even Drew's father says he thinks Kevin will milk this for all the attention he can get."

"So let's not give him any more of ours," Becca said.

Brie walked over and stood next to the bed. "When do you get out of this place? If I were you, I wouldn't be in too big of a hurry. I spied a very cute doctor in the hallway when I was coming in."

"I get out as soon as my not-too-cute doctor comes by and releases me."

Brie bent to smell a bouquet of mixed flowers David had sent, then paused to read the card. "Will you be going back to the Bluffs?" she asked.

"No. I'm checking into a motel."

"I can't let you do that," Brie protested. "Come and stay with Drew and me. I'll take care of you until you're completely recovered."

"You have far too much to do keeping up with your politician husband to take me on. Besides, I'll only be in the motel until I find a place. There have to be lots of apartments in this town for rent."

The phone rang. Becca reached over and answered it, half expecting it to be David, but it was Claire's voice that answered her hello. She covered the mouthpiece with her hand and whispered a quick apology to Brie for having to take the call while they were visiting.

"You sound upset, Claire. Is something wrong?"

"I've started to remember the night of the abduction."

"That's great. Isn't it?"

"It is, although it's got me so shaky I can barely function."

"Do you remember who kidnapped you?"

"Not yet, but I remember details not only about that night, but about the days immediately after that."

"What does your doctor say?"

"He wants to hypnotize me again. When he tried it before, I got so upset that he stopped the procedure, but now he thinks I'm ready."

"What do you think?"

"I want it over with. I want the man in jail so I can go on with my life and quit jumping at every shadow, stop thinking every man I meet is somehow connected to the abduction. The other night when Geoffrey saved us from being killed, I thought he was the man. And then when I went to the Bluffs, I was sure I could feel something evil about the place. Not necessarily David, but the house itself."

Catacombs with skulls and bones. Secret passageways and long tunnels. In the case of the Bluffs, Claire might not be altogether wrong, but Becca didn't want to bring that up now. "When do you see the doctor?"

"This afternoon. Wish me luck."

"I do, Claire. I wish you all the luck in the world."

Becca was still a little shaken by the conversation

even after they'd said their goodbyes and she'd hung up the phone.

"I take it that was Claire Cavendish," Brie said.

"It was."

Brie frowned. "She's started to remember things about the abduction. Did she tell you that?"

Since Brie knew that much, Becca saw no harm in telling her the rest. Brie listened attentively as she told about the hypnotism session scheduled for that afternoon.

"Poor girl." Brie turned to stare out the window. "So much to face. I suppose her mom's going with her to see the psychiatrist."

"No. The older kids are in school and her mom has the younger ones. But if Claire needs her after the session, Mrs. Cavendish will go to the doctor's office to pick her up as soon as Tommy gets in from school."

"It would be a miracle if Claire actually remembers the details of that night. I think it's the only way she'll ever move on." Brie squeezed Becca's hand. "And now I think I should get out of here and let you get some rest."

"That's all I've done for days. I'm eager to get back to Threads and sew."

GEOFFREY PIERCE STOOD outside Becca's hospital room, listening to the conversation between her and Brie. He'd decided to come by and pay a visit to the recovering victim, but he hadn't expected to learn so much without even talking to her.

Claire was getting her memory back. Becca was going on with her life. Or so they thought.

He hurried away as Brie wrapped up her visit. No need for him to be seen lurking in the hallway of the hospital, especially now that he'd already heard all he needed to know. Poor Claire. Poor Becca. Almost home free, then caught in the web.

DAVID SAT IN THE semidarkness of his catacomb retreat, feeling more and more like the subhuman freak the town saw him as. Becca had asked so little of him. So why hadn't he been able to bend a little?

He wanted Becca in his life, already longed to see her face across the table from him, to hear her laughter echoing through the Bluffs. He ached to touch her, to kiss her, to stretch out beside her in the four-poster bed and hold her in his arms and make love with her.

Instead he'd let her walk out of his life. Tense and heartsick, he went to the computer and opened Manning's files, scanning quickly back to September twenty years ago and the research project that had not been connected to any hospital or to the university. Subjects chosen from blood samples taken in routine physicals. The names of the women had been supplied by an unnamed contact in a local physician's office. Three women had been chosen—all having the elusive gene W. All suspected of being direct descendants of Moriah's Landing's infamous witch population.

And, of course, Joyce Telatia had been in that group of three. But who had been the doctor conducting the research?

He'd gone through all the doctors at that time, one by one, gone back and looked at their pictures. None had matched the description Joyce gave in her diary. Even Leland Manning had not checked out, though he'd thought at first that he might.

He picked up the phone and punched in the number of Becca's room at the hospital. At least he could check on her and see how she was doing, though he knew the real reason he was calling was just to hear her voice. The phone rang seven times before a floor nurse picked up and identified herself.

"I'm sorry, sir, Miss Smith has checked out of the hospital."

"Do you know where she went?"

"No, but I did see her talking to Geoffrey Pierce in front of the hospital. Perhaps he gave her a ride home."

Geoffrey Pierce. The name flashed across his brain as if it were lit in neon. Geoffrey had been a member of the secret society when David had first moved back to town, until he'd been voted out of the group five years ago. But he wasn't a doctor.

Geoffrey Pierce. Mid-forties now. That would have made him the right age then. The hair color was right. As for the rest of the description from Joyce's diary, it was difficult to tell. A man changed a lot in twenty years. But David had never trusted Geoffrey, always thought there was something inherently evil about the guy.

Could he have been the man that Joyce saw even though he wasn't qualified to supervise the complete project, even though he was not actually involved in medicine at all? Why not? The society never followed any other standard procedures.

Geoffrey Pierce, a murderer? The missing piece.

And Becca was with Geoffrey Pierce now. Panic ripped through him with the force of a cannonball. Running on gut instinct and an overload of adrenaline, he went to the gun closet, unlocked it and took the shiny pistol from the case. He had to find Becca now. If Geoffrey was the killer…

But in his mind, there was no "if." He knew it with the same certainty that he knew he loved Becca Smith.

Now all he had to do was find her in time. And once he did, he would never let her go.

BECCA OPENED HER EYES and stared at a bare lightbulb that seemed to be circling over her like a buzzard waiting for lunch. Her vision was blurry, her mind thick with an impenetrable fog. She tried to move but couldn't. Her arms were strapped to her sides, and her feet seemed leaden. She could hear breathing. Someone was nearby though she couldn't see who it was.

"Where am I?"

"We're in hell, Becca. Geoffrey Pierce's hell."

The voice infiltrated her consciousness. "Claire, is that you?"

"Yes. I'm only a few feet away to your right."

Becca struggled to rouse from the lassitude that claimed her body, finally managing to turn her head enough to see the bed through the drug-induced haze that glazed her eyes. Claire was laid out on a gurney, her hands and feet strapped down. She had needles embedded in both arms, attached to tubes that appeared to be extracting blood from her body in slow but steady trickles.

Geoffrey Pierce. Her memory slid in and out of focus, letting her retrieve bits and pieces of information. She'd run into him at the hospital and he'd offered her a ride to the motel. She'd refused, remembering what Claire had said about suspecting Geoffrey. But he'd injected her with something that had left her weak and woozy. He'd put her in his car and tied her hands and feet, but hadn't bothered to blindfold her as he'd taken back roads down the beach to the Pierces' beach house.

He'd carried her inside and down to his basement lab. And then—her mind went blank. No, there had been another needle, plunged deep into her vein, and she'd started falling, and falling and falling.

"How did you get here, Claire?"

"When I got out of my car at the doctor's office, Geoffrey was waiting for me. He'd come back for me to finish what he started five years ago. I think I always knew that he would."

"Oh, my God. Not Geoffrey. Surely it wasn't Drew's uncle who abducted and tortured you."

"But it was. He's the monster, and he's going to kill us both."

Becca closed her eyes and floated away, into the clear blue water. Her lungs hurt and the salt burned her throat and her eyes. She kicked and fought as hard as she could, but Geoffrey just kept holding her down. She was going to die.

She shook her head, trying in vain to escape the drugs' hold on her mind. She'd been in the hospital, not the water. "We're not going to die, Claire. We can't give up."

"I can. I want to die. Soon. Before he starts to touch me and hurt me the way he did before."

Her voice cracked and broke and she started to sob, a quiet, mournful sound that crawled inside Becca and squeezed at her heart. But still she didn't want to die. There had to be a way out. If she could only move. If she could only clear her mind.

GEOFFREY'S OWN BLOOD ran cold as he stared at the results of the blood test. It couldn't be, and yet it was. DNA didn't lie. Becca Smith was not Becca Smith at all. She was Tasha Pierce.

He'd never wanted to hurt Tasha, had never expected her to be on the boat that night. He'd realized too late that she was. When he found her still alive in the water after the explosion, he'd panicked, fearing she could tie him to the deed. He'd tried to drown her, and ended up strangling her. If he'd left her body to be found by the authorities, they'd have found the marks on her neck and known she was murdered.

Young and scared himself, he'd thrown her lifeless body in the trunk of his car and driven for hours, finally driving off the road in the middle of the night and burying her in a shallow grave he'd dug with a shovel he'd stolen from some farmer's barn.

Tasha Pierce was dead and buried. He knew that much for a fact. Whoever, whatever, lay in that room down the hall wasn't human. She not only had gene W, she had a witch's powers. His insides quivered and his stomach did a free fall, sinking and jerking inside him. He jumped from the chair and ran to the bathroom. He was going to be sick. He was going to be very, very sick.

And then he was going to destroy the nefarious, inhuman creature that lay in the next room.

A few minutes later, he wiped his mouth on the back of his shirtsleeve and walked to the room where Becca's body was strapped to the gurney.

"You shouldn't have come back, Tasha. You should have stayed dead."

I HAVE TO KILL YOU, TASHA. I have to kill you. Don't you see? I have no choice now.

The words rumbled around in her mind, a storm that threatened to wash her away. And then the images started. The boat. The explosion. The mounds of suffocating earth.

She tried to scream as the memories flooded her mind.

They were jumbled and mired in confusion, but they were there.

She was Tasha Pierce.

DAVID HAD RUSHED TO the Pierces' beach house, not sure what he'd find, or if he'd find anything at all. Geoffrey could have taken Becca anywhere.

He skidded to a stop in the front driveway, jumped out of the car and ran to the door. Amazingly it was unlocked, even ajar a few inches. Pulling the pistol from the shoulder holster, he stepped inside. As silently as he could, he walked from room to room, keeping his back to the wall, ready to pull the trigger at a split second's notice.

The house was richly furnished, the consummate bachelor's pad. Large pillows on the couch, a big-screen TV and elaborate music system. A plush, furry rug in front of the fireplace. Nothing was out of place, and there was no sign of Becca or anyone else.

He'd been so sure that Geoffrey was his man back at the Bluffs. Now the dulling throb of possibility began to pound against his temples. Had he been wrong? Stopping in the kitchen, he leaned against the marble counter.

A door squeaked open behind him. He jerked around as a sleek black cat crept through the door, stopped to look at him, then walked right past and crouched in the corner to watch him. David walked to the door and peered down a set of steep steps that disappeared into a dark hole. And from somewhere below him, he heard the sound of a toilet flushing.

A new wave of adrenaline exploded inside him as he headed down the steps. The smells were familiar. Antiseptics, formaldehyde, alcohol. Geoffrey wasn't a doctor, yet he had some kind of lab in his basement. The

elusive pieces of the jagged-edged puzzle began to fall
into place. Only now Becca was caught in the iron grips
of their claws.

And Geoffrey Pierce was a far more practiced killer
than Kevin Pinelle. He'd honed his craft two decades
ago.

"PLEASE, GEOFFREY. KILL ME. Please kill me."

Becca could hear Claire's voice, but it sounded as if
it were coming from deep within a bottomless pit. Becca
herself seemed to be floating somewhere far above
Claire, outside her own body. A gray shroud glazed her
eyes, and the room spun slowly through a heavy blanket
of fog. She tried to comfort Claire, but her tongue was
thick and refused to move in her dry mouth.

"I'll kill you, all right, Claire, in my own good time,
after I make you pay for escaping the first time. But
Tasha will have to die now. She's a witch, you know.
That's why I have to drain the blood from her body and
keep it pure. Once I find the secret of longevity, I'll no
longer be the poor Pierce relative, the one who never
quite lived up to the family's standard."

Becca tried to focus, but all she could make out was
shadows and streaks of light. Facts drifted in and out of
her mind. Geoffrey Pierce was her uncle, but he was
going to kill her. Was it because she loved David?

David. She closed her eyes and tried to pull up his
image. So handsome he took her breath away. He'd
kissed her on top of the Ferris wheel. She could feel his
lips on her now. Warm. Sweet. He took her in his arms
and they floated away. They'd be together always now.

"Okay, Miss Tasha. The fun is over. You have
enough phenobarbital in you now, you won't fight me

when I drain the blood from your body. I can't really kill you. I did that five years ago. You're already dead.''

DAVID FOLLOWED THE SOUND of Geoffrey's voice. The man was truly mad. Mad, but brilliant, so smart he'd gotten away with murder for twenty years. David would have to play it carefully, make certain there was no way for Geoffrey to get the upper hand. He was certain the man would kill both him and Becca without any hesitation.

David stopped just outside the door, took a deep breath, poised his trigger finger and pushed into the room where Geoffrey held Becca prisoner. ''The game's over, Geoffrey.''

''Well, look who came to the party. If it isn't Dr. David Bryson, the hideous beast who stole the Bluffs from me.''

David saw Claire first, then caught sight of Becca in the periphery of his vision. Anger erupted inside him, driving him so near the edge he thought he might be going mad himself. ''It's over, Pierce. Your days of killing women and getting away with it have come to an end.''

''You don't know anything about me.''

''I know you killed Joyce Telatia twenty years ago and the other two women, as well. For all I know you might have even had something to do with Kat's mother's murder.''

''No. I didn't kill her. I found her dead. I stole part of her blood, though I was too drunk to do it right.''

''You tampered with the dead and got a real taste for blood. Is that the way it happened, Geoffrey? And you liked it so well, you abducted Claire fifteen years later.''

''You think you're so smart, don't you, Dr. David

Bryson? But you don't know half the story. Once a man kills, he has to kill again and again. Only I wised up after Joyce Telatia. I waited months between each murder, then I went out of town, from town to town, found women of the night that no one missed, anyway. But I would never have come after Becca if she hadn't gotten mixed up with you and Claire. I warned her to stay away from you, in writing and in person. Too bad she didn't heed my warning.''

"But she didn't listen, so you tried to run her over the cliff.''

"Yes, but I didn't know then that I was trying to kill a dead woman. Now I do. She's dead, David. Dead.''

David stared at Becca. Her eyes had a blank, glazed sheen, and her arms hung limp at her sides. And in that second, he died a thousand deaths.

He raised the gun and pointed it at Geoffrey. The black cat sprang from nowhere, ran across the room and jumped on the top of Becca's stomach. Its back went up, and it snarled and extended its claws.

"Where did that damn witch cat come from?'' Geoffrey yelled as sweat broke out all over his body.

At that moment, Becca's body jerked, a series of quick movements, and then she turned her face toward David. His heart slammed against his chest so hard he wondered if it had stopped beating before. "Put your hands in the air, Geoffrey. Now. Or not. I'm aching for you to give me one reason to shoot.''

"Then go ahead.'' Geoffrey grabbed a syringe from the table and pointed the needle at Becca as if it were a dart. "A dose of cyanide and it's all over. All it has to do is seep into her muscle tissue.''

"Put that needle down, or so help me, I'll blow you away.''

The next thing David saw was the needle hurtling through space, heading straight for Becca. Geoffrey had struck the fatal blow, and there was nothing he could do to stop it.

Chapter Eighteen

David dived toward Becca in a futile attempt to shield her body with his, to take the cyanide for her. He was too late, but the black cat wasn't. She jumped at the needle, avoiding the point but causing it to ricochet and miss its mark. The point plunged into the floor beside the bed a second before David landed on top of Becca.

David turned back toward Geoffrey, the gun still in his hand, but Geoffrey had disappeared. David could hear his footsteps pounding on the steps that led back up the basement steps and into the house. A minute later he heard a loud yell and then the clunking and bumping of something clattering down the stairwell.

By the time he reached the steps, Geoffrey was lying at the bottom of them, clawing at his throat as his body shook and gyrated in convulsions. A hypodermic needle was jammed into his heart. Apparently he'd taken an extra injection with him just in case David had followed. But he'd never made the escape. He'd tripped on something and fallen, plunging the cyanide-filled needle into his heart.

The convulsions stopped. It was too late to help him. Geoffrey had been killed by his own poison.

David turned to see the black cat sitting in the shadows, licking her paws and purring. He checked Geoffrey's pulse just to be certain the man was dead. There was none. When he looked around, the cat had disappeared.

David hurried back to Becca. He held her in his arms for painful minutes before he could make himself let go of her long enough to call an ambulance. When he finished the call, he stopped at Claire's gurney and whispered words of reassurance to her before taking Becca in his arms again.

"I know you're too out of it to understand right now, but I love you, Becca, more than life itself. I want to spend the rest of my life with you if you'll have me. I don't want to live in the past. I just want to love you."

"It's okay, David. I'm Tasha." Her words were slurred, her tongue thick from drugs, her voice no louder than a whisper. He wasn't sure what she said, other than that it was something about Tasha.

"Don't try to talk now, Becca. Just know how much I love you."

But she opened her mouth again and he put his ear close to her mouth so she wouldn't have to strain.

"I'm home, David. I'm finally home."

THE FALL EXTRAVAGANZA was everything the people of Moriah's Landing could have dreamed of—music, food, people dressed in costumes of the days when Moriah's Landing was founded. The temperature was in the high sixties, the air brisk and carrying the scent of pumpkins and late fall blossoms. The sky was clear, alive with sparkling stars and a full harvest moon. The mysteries that had haunted the town for the last twenty years were solved, and now Geoffrey Pierce lay in the cemetery, not far from the grave of McFarland Leary.

David still woke up every morning trying to convince himself all over again that his new life wasn't a dream. He held Tasha's hand as they walked through the crowd and toward the back of the gazebo where they were to meet Drew and Brie. They never made more than a few steps' progress without someone stopping to hug her and tell her how glad they were to have her back.

Amazingly enough, a lot of them shook his hand, as well, and thanked him for his part in stopping not one but two killers. His status of town beast was slipping fast, but he had to admit he liked his new status of hero much better. Even the scar appeared to be growing on people, and it bothered him less and less every day, as did the rest of his mangled body. Tasha loved him, and that was good enough for him.

Tasha. He still had trouble getting used to calling her that after she'd been Becca in his mind for the last few months. He loved the woman she'd become as much as he loved the one he'd met and fallen in love with five years ago. But knowing that she was the same woman explained the immediate and overwhelming attraction they'd had for each other from that first brief moment when their eyes had met.

"Looks like the whole gang is waiting on us," Tasha said, waving. "Drew and Brie, Kat and Jonah, and Elizabeth and Cullen."

"Claire's with them, too."

Tasha strained her neck. "I don't see Claire."

"Standing next to Elizabeth."

"Oh, my gosh, that is her. She looks absolutely stunning. It's hard to imagine her as the frightened mouse of a woman that she was just a few short weeks ago."

"And speaking of stunning, did I tell you how wonderful you look tonight?"

She put a finger to her chin flirtatiously. "I'm not sure. Better tell me again just in case."

"No. You're getting much too spoiled." But he kissed her and knew he was the one leading the charmed life.

TASHA, ELIZABETH, KAT, BRIE and Claire sat at a table under the stars while the men in their lives stood in line for a round of drinks.

"I never thought we'd all be together again like this," Brie said, tugging on the puffed sleeves of her dress. "Now that we are, I'm having trouble believing it."

Elizabeth spread her hands on the table, her diamond engagement ring that accompanied her wedding band reflecting the sparkle from the strings of miniature lights strung over their heads. "We've come a long way from that night five years ago in the cemetery."

"I had to travel back from hell," Claire said. "I couldn't have done it without all of you."

Kat reached over and squeezed her hand. "I just wish I could have done more."

"I guess most of the thanks goes to David Bryson," Brie said. "If it hadn't been for him, Tasha would have been killed without our ever having known that she hadn't died in the explosion the night before her wedding."

"I love him," Tasha said.

"Like we haven't noticed," Brie said as they all started laughing. "You drool all over the man."

"Well, he is the hero of the day. Not only did he save my and Claire's lives, but he may have developed a drug that can save Brie's mother's life."

"I'm keeping my fingers crossed," Brie said.

"We all are," they agreed in unison.

"It's been some year for Moriah's Landing," Elizabeth said. "Murders, underhanded medical schemes, scams of all descriptions. It's as if the evil finally crawled out of the old mansions and beat-up shacks along the wharves and got stamped under the feet of justice. And it's touched each one of us in some unique way."

"I'm still not clear on how it all fits together," Brie mused.

Elizabeth said, "It's like this—"

"The layman's version, Elizabeth," Brie interrupted. "No university criminology technical jive."

"You got it." Elizabeth smoothed the tablecloth, ready to illustrate with the cocktail forks and napkins the scenario as she saw it. "Geoffrey Pierce, Dr. Leland Manning and even before him, Dr. Rathfastar, were all part of the secret medical society, all searching for the elusive gene W that they thought existed in the original witches of Moriah's Landing. Dr. Rathfastar was too radical for the other members and they dismissed him from the group."

"Kicked him right out," Kat said, taking away one of the forks Elizabeth had lined up across the center of the table. "And that pissed the guy off."

"Big time," Elizabeth agreed. "So he started grabbing Manning's subjects and killing them, taking the blood for his own experiments and not leaving any blood in the body for Manning. That's why when Rathfastar was arrested, the crime spree wasn't fully over."

"And that's when my Jonah stepped in," Kat said.

"He stopped the illegal medical supplies—or rather, mummified corpses—that a member of the secret society was bringing into the county. And during his investigation, we found out that Ernie McDougal was the man who killed my mother twenty years ago.'' Kat took away another fork.

"And then came a new villain," Brie said. "Dr. Leland Manning, the monster who tried to do experiments on my daughter. And who killed his own wife and tried to kill Drew." She picked up a fork.

"And finally Geoffrey Pierce. Strange how it all runs full circle," Tasha said, picking up all the forks and holding them in the circle of her right hand. "All the searching for gene W and I have it. So now we know that there's nothing to the theory that drove so many men to such heinous crimes."

"I wouldn't be too sure," Claire said. "You've cheated death five times now. The night of the explosion, being buried alive, the crash on Old Mountain Road, the knife of Kevin Pinelle and the cyanide-laced needle of Geoffrey Pierce."

A shudder rippled up Tasha's backbone and she let the forks drop to the table with a clatter. "You don't really think I'm a witch, do you?"

"Of course not." Elizabeth said. "Just one lucky woman."

"Let's join hands," Kat said, "the way we did that night at the cemetery. Only this time we'll all think of all the things that bind us as friends."

"Friends forever," Tasha said, taking the hands of Brie and Claire. They closed their eyes and Tasha let her mind float from one to the other of the women at the table. She was so lucky to have friends like this, fortunate to have found her way back to Moriah's Landing and the people who loved her. The moment seemed to pass in an instant, but they all held on to one another's hands until the men returned, no one willing to break the bond that held them.

Friends forever. Lucky in love. Fortunate to be alive.

"IT WAS A PERFECT NIGHT," Tasha said, slipping inside David's arms.

"Almost perfect," David agreed.

She propped a hand on her hip seductively, and his heart rolled over inside him.

"We could make it perfect," she teased, "once we get back to the Bluffs. Are you ready to go?"

"Not quite." He tugged her beneath a cover of twinkling lights that threaded around the bare branches of an oak tree.

"You look so serious," she said, her eyes shining as brightly as the lights. "You're not about to dump me, are you?"

"Not in this lifetime, but I am serious." He fumbled in his front pocket for the ring, making sure it was still there. He'd done this five years ago, but he was certain he couldn't have been any more nervous then than he was now.

He took her left hand in his and got down on one knee. "I loved you as Tasha and I loved you as Becca Smith." He had practiced a flowery speech. He couldn't remember a word of it now. "Will you marry me?"

She fell to her knees beside him. "We never made it to the altar, but I married you with my heart and soul five years ago, David Bryson, and our love was so strong that it drew me back to Moriah's Landing even though I couldn't remember the place or you." She cradled his face in her hands, and he could see the moisture glistening in her eyes. "It's always been you. It always will be."

"Is that a yes?"

She wrapped her arms around him and kissed him. "It's a yes."

He stood and tugged her to her feet. "Should I ask your parents' permission again?"

"Let's just ask their blessing, David. And I'm sure they'll give it. Since you saved my life, twice, they're ready to nominate you for man of the year. Drew, too. As soon as he's elected mayor, he'll probably give you the keys to the city."

"I don't need a key to the city. I have everything I need right here in my arms tonight." He slipped the ring on her finger, and the tears she'd held in check started to roll down her cheek. He kissed them away as the band started playing. The beautiful, haunting theme from *Beauty and the Beast* wafted across the green.

"May I have this dance?" he whispered, his mouth close to her ear. "They're playing our song. Just don't expect me to turn into the handsome prince."

"You already have."

An owl hooted somewhere overhead. Tasha trembled, instinctively, afraid that the owl was an omen that their happiness would be ripped away from them again. But David took her in his arms and held her close as they moved to the music. The fear was swept away in the magic of the moment. Love was the only omen she'd believe in anymore.

A love that had lived inside both of them and drawn them back together against all odds. Claire had been right all along. She was bewitched by David, and he by her. He lowered his mouth to hers, and she lost herself in his kiss.

Bewitched forevermore.

Coming in July!
Top Harlequin® Presents author

Sandra Marton

Brings you a brand-new, spin-off
to her miniseries, *The Barons*

Raising the Stakes

**Attorney Gray Baron has come to Las Vegas on a mission to find
a woman—Dawn Lincoln Kittredge—the long-lost grandchild of
his uncle Jonas Baron. And when he finds her, an undeniable
passion ignites between them.**

A powerful and dramatic read!

Look for it in stores, July 2002.

If you enjoyed what you just read,
then we've got an offer you can't resist!

Take 2 bestselling love stories FREE!

Plus get a FREE surprise gift!

Clip this page and mail it to Harlequin Reader Service®

IN U.S.A.	IN CANADA
3010 Walden Ave.	P.O. Box 609
P.O. Box 1867	Fort Erie, Ontario
Buffalo, N.Y. 14240-1867	L2A 5X3

YES! Please send me 2 free Harlequin Intrigue® novels and my free surprise gift. After receiving them, if I don't wish to receive anymore, I can return the shipping statement marked cancel. If I don't cancel, I will receive 4 brand-new novels each month, before they're available in stores! In the U.S.A., bill me at the bargain price of $3.80 plus 25¢ shipping and handling per book and applicable sales tax, if any*. In Canada, bill me at the bargain price of $4.21 plus 25¢ shipping and handling per book and applicable taxes**. That's the complete price and a savings of at least 10% off the cover prices—what a great deal! I understand that accepting the 2 free books and gift places me under no obligation ever to buy any books. I can always return a shipment and cancel at any time. Even if I never buy another book from Harlequin, the 2 free books and gift are mine to keep forever.

181 HEN DC7U
381 HEN DC7V

Name	(PLEASE PRINT)	
Address	Apt.#	
City	State/Prov.	Zip/Postal Code

* Terms and prices subject to change without notice. Sales tax applicable in N.Y.
** Canadian residents will be charged applicable provincial taxes and GST.
All orders subject to approval. Offer limited to one per household and not valid to current Harlequin Intrigue® subscribers.
® are registered trademarks of Harlequin Enterprises Limited.

INT01

A ROYAL MONARCH'S SEARCH FOR AN HEIR LEADS TO DANGER IN:

The Carradignes: A Royal Mystery

from

HARLEQUIN®

INTRIGUE®

Plain-Jane royal secretary Ellie Standish wanted one night to shine. But when she was mistaken for a princess and kidnapped by masked henchmen, this dressed-up Cinderella had only one man to turn to—one of her captors: a dispossessed duke who had his own agenda to protect her and who ignited a fire in her soul. Could Ellie trust this man with her life…and her heart?

Don't miss:
THE DUKE'S COVERT MISSION
JULIE MILLER   June 2002

And check out these other titles in the series

The Carradignes: American Royalty

available from HARLEQUIN AMERICAN ROMANCE:

THE IMPROPERLY PREGNANT PRINCESS
JACQUELINE DIAMOND   March 2002

THE UNLAWFULLY WEDDED PRINCESS
KARA LENNOX   April 2002

THE SIMPLY SCANDALOUS PRINCESS
MICHELE DUNAWAY   May 2002

And coming in November 2002:
THE INCONVENIENTLY ENGAGED PRINCE
MINDY NEFF

Available at your favorite retail outlet.

HARLEQUIN®

Makes any time special ®

Visit us at www.eHarlequin.com

HICR